THE PLACE OF MUSIC:
ESSAYS FROM THE FIRST DECADE
OF THE BARD COLLEGE
CONSERVATORY OF MUSIC

EDITED BY ROBERT MARTIN

The Place of Music: Essays from the First Decade of the
Bard College Conservatory of Music

Copyright © 2016 Bard College Conservatory of Music

Cover by R. O. Blechman
Al fresco consort of spinet, lute, recorder, and bass viol.
Anonymous Italian painting, sixteenth century. Musée de Bourges.
Erich Lessing/Art Resource, NY.

This publication has been produced by the Bard College Publications Office:
Mary Smith, Director
Ann Gabler, Project Director
Karen Walker Spencer, Designer
Debby Mayer, Copy Editor

All rights reserved. Except in reviews and critical articles, no part of
this book may be used or reproduced in any manner without written
permission from Bard College Conservatory of Music.

Acknowledgments
Grateful acknowledgment is given to reprint the following articles.
"Musical 'Topics' and Expression in Music" by Robert Martin is reprinted
from *The Journal of Aesthetics and Art Criticism*, Vol. 53, No. 4 (Autumn 1995)
published by Wiley on behalf of The American Society for Aesthetics.

"'Nothing Is Too Good for the Working Class': Classical Music,
the High Arts and Workers' Culture" by John Halle is reprinted from
New Politics Vol. XIV No. 4 Whole Number 56, Winter 2014.

ISBN: 978-1-936192-51-9

Published by
Bard College Conservatory of Music
PO Box 5000
Annandale-on-Hudson, NY 12504-5000
bard.edu/conservatory

Contents

Preface

ROBERT MARTIN

The idea for this volume came first from the desire to celebrate a milestone—a decade since the founding of the Bard Conservatory in 2005—but a milestone that by itself is of interest mainly to us insiders. Of broader interest is the unusual nature of the Bard Conservatory. As the only conservatory requiring completion of a Bachelor of Arts degree in a field other than music simultaneous with the awarding of the Bachelor of Music degree, the Bard Conservatory's first decade of experience with that requirement, along with other innovations, invites reflection and evaluation. Why should young musicians have a broad, liberal arts education? Will it improve them as musicians? Will they have enough time to practice? What does the Bard experience mean for the future?

Part I, The Conservatory, addresses these questions through two of my essays, the first a brief history of the Conservatory emphasizing the challenges it faced and the strategies it marshaled, and the second, "On the Education of Musicians: A Manifesto," on its philosophy. That second essay also offers a suggestion as to how the traditional view—that gifted young musicians should focus almost entirely on music alone—developed historically and became prevalent. Part I also includes essays meant to give a vivid sense of the life of the Conservatory, by soprano Dawn Upshaw, founding artistic director of our Graduate Vocal Arts Program; cellist Rylan Gajek-Leonard '16, written while still an undergraduate student at the Conservatory; and pianist Allegra Chapman '10, a member of our first graduating class.

Part II, Connections, is based on a fundamental part of the ideology of the Bard Conservatory, the belief that music is deeply and strongly connected with history, literature, science, architecture, social justice, philosophy, film, politics—in fact, all other aspects of life and thought. In keeping with this belief, we asked a group of friends and colleagues to present us with essays on music's connections. The resulting eclectic mix—almost all written specifically for this volume—constitutes Part II.

In an essay on the philosophy of music, I examine the idea of musical "topics" as a solution to the philosophical problem of expression in music, and defend a different approach to that problem via the notion of expressive playing.

André Aciman writes on "folding and refolding," a notion he takes from Julia Child's *Mastering the Art of French Cooking*—"the equivalent, say, of treading water without budging in a swimming pool"—and finds it applicable to Beethoven, Joyce, and Proust.

The conductor Ádám Fischer reflects on the torture and murder of Sinti and Roma at Auschwitz in October 1944, and the duty of artists, and civil society in general, to remember such events.

Jerrold Seigel discusses music's relationship to neighboring domains of culture in nineteenth-century Europe, the time when the modern sense of the term culture became firmly established.

Peter Laki and Swapan S. Jain look at the two sides of Alexander Borodin: the composer of the opera *Prince Igor* was also the chemist who identified a reaction of silver carboxylate salts with liquid bromine, known now as the Borodin-Hunsdiecker reaction. He was also a champion of women's education in science and medicine.

Robert Kelly, writing on the relation between words and music, suggests to the composer: "Let the words die into the music" and "Let them lead to sounds, let sentences lead to song, the urgent paragraph or stanza lead to aria."

Deborah Berke reflects on the kinds of spaces that a school of music needs, and the ways in which the work of the architect is similar to the work of the musician.

John Halle asks whether the "high arts" have a place within a social movement for working people. He pursues the question historically, considering such figures as Hans Eisler and Charles Seeger, and the role of the labor unions in the United States.

Melvin Chen compares the ways in which performers and scientists synthesize information, and also considers work in evolutionary biology on art in the natural world.

R. O. Blechman writes on connections with rhythm and time in the creation of his animated film version of Stravinsky's *The Soldier's Tale*.

I gratefully acknowledge the expert and dedicated work of my colleagues Ann Gabler, Mary Smith, Debby Mayer, and Karen Spencer.

PART I

THE CONSERVATORY

A Brief History of the Bard Conservatory

ROBERT MARTIN

The decision to move ahead toward a Bard Conservatory of Music was made on May 7, 2002 at a gala dinner for Bard's Center for Curatorial Studies. There I found myself alone in conversation with Bard president Leon Botstein, an unusual occurrence at such events. When Leon asked if I was enjoying myself at Bard I said yes, and I wondered what he would think about the idea of creating our own Conservatory at Bard. He replied at once that it was a good idea, and I should take some time to visit other conservatories to see how we could create something truly distinctive.

It was no coincidence that I was attracted to the idea of the combination of a music conservatory and a college or university. I had attended the Curtis Institute of Music and Haverford College together over a five-year period, earning a bachelor of music degree in cello performance and a bachelor of arts degree in philosophy. It had been a wonderful experience for me, but it could have been improved by coordination between the two institutions, or better yet, by the existence of the two programs within one institution. Bard seemed perfect not only because its president is a world-class musician and because it was just completing construction of a major performance venue—The Richard B. Fisher Center for the Performing Arts—but also because Bard has a history of bold and innovative educational initiatives.

Two years later, on May 21, 2004, the trustees of the College approved a formal proposal: ". . . to create a small conservatory on the Bard College campus—known as the Conservatory at Bard College—in which all students pursue not only the traditional conservatory degree (bachelor of music) but also the bachelor of arts degree in a field other than music. Such a program, in which no separate bachelor of music degree is offered, would be unique in the United States today."

Research and Recruiting

In the two years between the birth of the idea and the approval of its creation, there were four particularly crucial ingredients: research on other conservatories, the participation of Melvin Chen, recruiting of faculty, and the shaping of a distinctive curriculum.

In the summer of 2002 I met with Michael Mandaren, director of admission at the Oberlin Conservatory. and several of its faculty. The Oberlin Conservatory was founded in 1867, only two years after the founding of the distinguished liberal arts college, and the two have been fully unified ever since.

At the Oberlin Conservatory students may pursue a five-year, double-degree program toward the Conservatory degree and the Oberlin College B.A. degree—an obvious model for our program. Mandaren was gracious and helpful in answering my questions. I learned that Oberlin's double-degree program is its signature program: approximately 70 percent of all applicants express interest in pursuing it. I also learned that, generally speaking, the liberal arts faculty are very favorable toward the idea of admitting Conservatory double-degree applicants, and the Conservatory faculty less enthusiastic. Given the choice between two applicants of approximately equal musical ability, the Conservatory faculty member is likely to prefer the one who wishes to study only at the Conservatory. The reason given is that the former student is likely to be "distracted" from the study of music, and / or to decide to pursue a non-music career, in which case the investment will not have paid off. Tellingly, only about 15 percent of students graduating from the Conservatory complete the double-degree program, even though a far higher percentage begin in it. Faculty seem to regard the double degree as very difficult and definitely not suitable for most students.

I also visited the Shepherd School of Music of Rice University, and studied the programs of the other school noted for its five-year double-degree program, Lawrence University in Appleton, Wisconsin, as well as those of the New England Conservatory, Eastman School of Music, The Juilliard School, and the schools of music associated with large universities such as the University of Michigan, Indiana University, and the University of Southern California. I arrived at two conclusions: (1) double-degree students in all of these schools tend to feel marginal and isolated, and (2) bias against the double-degree program is part of the culture of these institutions, at least in part because most of the faculty are graduates of traditional conservatory programs that focus only on music.

I concluded that the Bard Conservatory should adopt the policy that the double-degree program be required, not optional. Our students would thereby not be marginal, and indeed might be likely to support and help each other. New students would learn from the experiences of more advanced students. Furthermore, faculty, having agreed to teach at the Bard Conservatory and knowing our policy, would be likely to resist the inclination to counsel students toward an exclusive focus on music studies.

Melvin Chen joined the Bard faculty in the fall of 2001, teaching both in the Music Program and in a variety of programs in the Division of Science, Mathematics, and Computing. We first met when he performed in the 2000 Bard Music Festival. I was impressed by his performances and by his education: B.S. from Yale in physics and chemistry, M.M. from Juilliard in piano and violin, Ph.D. in chemistry from Harvard. Melvin and I became good friends. Once the idea of the Bard Conservatory was born, we talked endlessly about every aspect of how it might work. He was an obvious poster child for the guiding double-degree idea. In February 2004, when Melvin was in his third year of teaching at Bard, and I was preparing the proposal to Bard's Board of Trustees to launch the Conservatory, I invited Melvin to become associate director of the Conservatory, a position he held until he left in 2012 to become professor of piano and deputy dean of the Yale School of Music.

Melvin had a strong influence on the shaping of the Bard Conservatory, for at least three reasons. First, he was very good at seeing the implications of seemingly small decisions that we needed to make—seeing the precedents that would be set and the difficulties that might arise from various choices. Second, he had a very clear sense of how prospective and current students would react to policy decisions we might make, partly, I suppose, because he was fairly close in age to those students. Third, he had a range of contacts in the music world quite different from mine, again because of age; it helped that he was liked and admired by all who knew him. This was of enormous help in recruiting faculty and finding strategies for recruiting students. Beyond these three qualities, however, it was simply the extremely high level of Melvin's achievement and the high standards to which he held himself that made the most difference to the life of the Conservatory.

The recruiting of an extraordinary faculty was perhaps the most important factor in the early and continued success of the Conservatory.

Robert Fitzpatrick, then dean at Curtis Insitute of Music, filled me in on the details of their audition process, financial arrangements with faculty, support for students traveling to New York City for lessons, arrangements for orchestra and chamber music, and many other matters. He led me to see that the roster system for faculty—paid by the hour for lessons actually given—would serve us well, just as it did Curtis. The Manhattan School and Mannes College, both in New York City, also operated on the roster system, which seemed to suit busy artists whose availability and priorities were liable to change frequently.

I spoke first with pianist Richard Goode, whom I knew from our years of study together, first at Marlboro and then at the Curtis Institute. Richard did not, and still does not, teach on a regular basis at any school, but he agreed to join our roster to give master classes on a regular basis. His agreement, even on that limited basis, was very helpful in further recruiting.

Then followed meetings with many wonderful musicians, some of whom I knew from Curtis (Arnold Steinhardt and Michael Tree from the Guarneri Quartet, pianist Peter Serkin) and others from various previous encounters in the music world (violinists Laurie Smukler, Ida Kavafian, and Ani Kavafian; violist Ira Weller; cellist Peter Wiley, and many others). In every case I offered several features that seemed attractive: they would teach only students whom they wished to teach; if their schedule did not permit trips to Bard, ninety minutes north of New York City, then we would send the student to New York City for lessons; and when they did come to Bard to teach, we would supplement their schedules with chamber music coaching, paid at the same hourly rate as the individual lessons. Above all, I promised that the students would be interesting, intelligent, and highly motivated. Some asked why the double degree was mandatory instead of optional; my answer, as explained above, seemed to satisfy them, and I had an almost 100 percent success rate in recruiting the faculty we wanted.

Melvin Chen was very helpful in faculty recruiting. He knew, far better than I, the musicians of his generation, and he was able to steer me to many superb players and teachers whom I would not have known otherwise (for example, flutist Tara Helen O'Connor). Another good source of faculty was the American Symphony Orchestra: clarinetist Laura Flax, trumpeter Carl Albach, and French hornist Jeffrey Lang came through that route.

Our goal was to find artist-teachers of a very special kind for the roster. We asked ourselves who—among those based in New York City or relatively near Bard, and whose artistry we admired—would attract students of the highest level? We understood that most gifted and advanced young players, and their parents, knew the teachers at the various conservatories and had dreams and preferences as to whom they would like to study with. It is no accident that many teachers we recruited also teach at Curtis or Juilliard. Where we were less familiar with the scene, as for example in the case of French horn, we inquired broadly of young professionals, "Who is the most distinguished horn teacher in the United States?" Then I arranged visits with these people and was, very fortunately, able to recruit them to join our roster.

Recruitment in China

Early on it was clear to us that China would be an important area for student recruiting. The other top conservatories all had large numbers of string and piano students from China, gifted and ambitious young musicians eager to come to the United States. This presented us with an immediate problem: How would these students fare with the double-degree program, since in many cases their English language skills were weak? Would they even consider a program such as ours, since the top music high schools in China were famous for encouraging students to focus on music to the almost complete exclusion of their other studies?

To help us answer these questions we turned to our friend, the violinist Weigang Li, founding first violinist of the Shanghai String Quartet. Weigang had attended the famous middle school attached to the Shanghai Conservatory and had maintained close connections throughout China since coming to the West. After hearing our plans and learning of our faculty, Weigang gave us his opinion: there would indeed be excellent students in China who, if offered the chance to study with the teachers on our roster, with very attractive financial aid, and with the understanding that they would also have to pursue the B.A. degree with a second major, would come to Bard. Many parents would be delighted to have their children get a broad education, he said, and the level of discipline and hard work of these students was generally high enough to make our program possible for them. And, we would need to offer intensive instruction in English as a Second Language.

Weigang Li's predictions were correct, and it was also greatly to our advantage that he agreed to join our faculty roster from the beginning. Not only did he attract students from China (and elsewhere), but he spoke directly with prospects and their families to explain our program, give assurances, and, in many cases, get information about the student's motivation that helped us make admission decisions. He was joined on our roster by another member of the Shanghai Quartet, Yiwen Jiang, who had studied and maintained contacts at the music high school attached to the Central Conservatory of Music in Beijing, and who helped us in similar ways.

While recruiting faculty we also worked at constructing the curriculum of the Conservatory. We used part of a planning grant of $50,000 from the Mellon Foundation to retain the composer Edward Harsh to study the curriculum and requirements of a wide array of conservatories and schools of music in the United States and to provide us with an analysis of the range of decisions to be made. His work, and our own discussions, including those with Leon Botstein, led to a number of important decisions about our curriculum. One was that the teaching of music theory needed to be changed significantly so that it was relevant to the actual performance of music. Another was that music theory should be integrated with relevant parts of music history. We also decided early on that every student in the Conservatory would have a least one semester of composition, as a capstone to the theory sequence and with the aim of deepening the performers' understanding of the process resulting in the composition of musical works. We decided also on an emphasis on chamber music.

Preparation of materials for publicizing the Conservatory and recruiting students required that we settle on a mission statement and many matters of fine-tuning the "message" that we wished to convey. The question was forced on us: Whom exactly were we intending to train, and what outcomes did we seek? We agreed that we wanted to convey the importance of a broad education without in any way downplaying the importance of focused dedication to music. Melvin Chen wrote the following, which we decided to use as a kind of preamble to the mission statement:

> *Music, like all art, engages the mind and the heart. It redefines boundaries and questions limits in order to make a meaningful statement about the human condition. The education of the mind is, therefore, as important as the education of the fingers. The greatest musicians not only have the technical mastery to communicate effectively, but also are deeply curious and equally adept at analytical and emotional modes of thought.*

Our mission statement simply assumes the correctness of that view as to the importance of a liberal arts education: *The mission of the Bard College Conservatory of Music is to provide the best possible preparation for a person dedicated to a life immersed in the creation and performance of music.*

Our recruiting materials seek to appeal to two very different audiences (and those in between): on the one hand, those who are strongly drawn to a conservatory-only model, for example Curtis and Juilliard, and who need to be convinced that Bard will provide what they are looking for *in addition* to a college education; on the other hand, those excellent players who are strongly drawn to fine and prestigious universities and colleges, and need to be convinced that Bard will provide what they are looking for *in addition* to conservatory training at the highest level.

Challenges

Because Melvin Chen and I were so enthusiastic about the double-degree concept and had so much enjoyed our own integrated studies as undergraduates, we may have underestimated the difficulty of recruiting to the Bard Conservatory. Another way to put it is that we overestimated the size of the pool for recruiting: those who played well enough to be admitted to the top conservatories and who also could be drawn to see the value of a liberal arts education. We put a lot of thought into framing our message to reach that relatively small group. Over the years I worked on many presentations trying to make the case for the double-degree program: that it would actually help the student become a better musician. In 2012, when I had the opportunity to address a plenary session of the Association of European Conservatories of Music, I consolidated those presentations into an essay, "On the Education of Musicians: A Manifesto," included in this volume.

Once the trustees of Bard College officially approved the new Conservatory in May 2004, with a projected opening date of the fall of 2005, we set out to recruit the first group of students. That summer I visited many festivals and schools in the United States, and in late November and December 2004 Melvin Chen and I traveled to Taiwan, South Korea, and China. In each place we visited leading arts high schools, offering master classes in some places, meeting with faculty and administrators, and hearing students whenever possible.

The situation in each country was different. In Shanghai, for example, there was sensitivity about having us hold auditions at the Middle School attached to the Shanghai Conservatory, even though many teachers there were eager to help their students arrange to study abroad. As a result, we were invited to join the auditions for a summer program in Canada, and then to speak informally with students who seemed good candidates for Bard. As a result of our visits to Shanghai and Beijing, eight students from China were recruited to start Bard in the fall of 2005. The opening class that fall consisted of 21 students: 10 from China, 8 from the United States, and one each from Germany, Malaysia, and Canada. Our recruiting continued throughout the spring and even into the summer.

Looking back, certain patterns emerged early on. Two of our first students—oboist Rachel Steinhorn, from the Chicago area, and clarinetist Sam Israel, from New Jersey—were players of conservatory quality but headed in the direction of science. They were perhaps not sure of that direction as 18-year-olds, and they took their music studies very seriously. Sam became one of the Biology Program's top students, and Rachel became one of the Psychology Program's top students. After five years of study and two degrees, Sam went on to a Ph.D. program in biochemistry at the University of California, Berkeley; Rachel went on to the Washington University School of Medicine in St. Louis. Of the other 19 students in that group, almost all went on to graduate school in music. A spirit of adventure and the realization that they were part of something new and significant held that group together.

On one of the first evenings of that first semester we held a pizza and chamber music party: all of the students, Melvin Chen, and I, and violinist Weigang Li, who was already known to the eight Chinese students. We collected stacks of music, some of it purchased just days before the start of the semester, moved tables and brought in stands and chairs into four or five rooms, and quickly organized ensembles: a Mendelssohn Octet, a Dvořák string quintet, an Ibert woodwind piece, and various piano trios. It was a fine ice-breaking and bonding experience and, in a peculiar way, an unrepeatable experience, for only in the first year of the Conservatory would *all* the students arrive, meet for the first time, and begin school together. In subsequent years we had only the new students for the first three weeks—generally too few for a real chamber music party—and they eagerly awaited the arrival of the returning older students. New patterns of bonding and socialization developed in those subsequent years, quite effective and interesting in themselves, but the memory of that first pizza and chamber music party is a very special one.

International Students and English-language Proficiency

It was clear at once that English language proficiency would be a large and continuing problem for the Conservatory. On the one hand, the eight students from China—violinists, violists, and pianists—were, as a group, the strongest players in the Conservatory. Within weeks we had performances both within Bard and in outside engagements that amazed the audiences. On the other hand, it was difficult to imagine how most of these eight Chinese students would survive academically. Their writing, especially, was weak. The story was always the same: the teachers at their excellent music high schools in China had told them to focus only on their music studies and to pay as little attention as possible to their other studies, including English. Once we got to know these students—their talent, achievement, and discipline, as well as their sense of humor, charm, and integrity—we couldn't imagine the Conservatory without them (and more like them), but at the same time, we knew we had a problem on our hands.

The first step had to do with College admissions. Bard's Admission Office had (and has) a liberal policy with respect to international students in general, deemphasizing the standardized Test of English as a Foreign Language (TOEFL) and looking at individual applicants on a case-by-case basis. Still, it was essential to Admission that applicants be able to succeed in the required First-Year Seminar, and it was clear that our Chinese applicants could not. Mary Backlund, director of admission, helpfully suggested that we make use of an Exception Admit status by which students were fully matriculated but needed to make up deficiencies by the end of their first year, proceeding thereafter as regular admits. Our Exception Admit students would postpone taking the First-Year Seminar until their second year. During the first year we would provide them with an English as a Second Language (ESL) course.

All first-year Bard students arrive three weeks before the returning students to take the three-week Workshop in Language and Thinking. This is a wonderful Bard replacement for the usual few days of orientation for first-year students. It was instituted some 35 years ago and is now a core part of the Bard experience, in which students not only focus on writing skills but also learn their way around campus and form new friendships before the start of school. The workshop involves a large dose of sophisticated reading material and very active class participation in small groups. It was, of course, important to have Conservatory students participate in the workshop, but the group from China would have been lost.

Fortunately, I had near at hand a perfect solution! Katherine Gould-Martin, the managing director of Bard in China, agreed to teach a section of L&T (as it was known) consisting, that year, of the eight students from China. (In subsequent years her section included other Exception Admit students, notably from Hungary, the Czech Republic, Poland, Venezuela, South Korea, and Ukraine). Katherine came up with many ingenious and effective ways to provide the essential elements of the L&T program for these students, using small pieces of the readings and relying occasionally on explanations in Chinese. Thanks to her and to the eagerness of most of the students, the program was a great success.

Once the academic year began, the Conservatory engaged an outside teacher for the special ESL class. This was, and has continued to be, a difficult class to teach: students' level varied widely, and they were easily distracted by their musical activities combined, perhaps, with their sense that this was not a "real" course. Bard's professor of Chinese language and literature, Li-hua Ying, came to our rescue midway through the first year and took over the ESL class. In our first 10 years we have had five different ESL teachers, each devoted and excellent, and each reporting frustrations and difficulties.

The first near-catastrophe occurred at the start of the Conservatory's second year, in the fall of 2006, when the first group of Exception Admit students (all from China) enrolled in First-Year Seminar (FYS), one year late as planned, mixed in with regular first-year students in various sections of the course. Several of the FYS instructors raised concerns with the dean about the English-language proficiency of the Chinese students, asking what was expected of them as instructors and expressing frustration with the teaching situation. Since these students had already completed a year of ESL and were already a year late in taking FYS, and since the Conservatory was new, the situation was genuinely worrisome. Melvin Chen and I did feel that the reported difficulties were given special weight because the faculty and the dean considered them systemic—arising from the creation of the Conservatory—rather than simply as those normally encountered in the course of teaching.

When the problem reached the attention of Leon Botstein, he proposed a striking solution. Since the U.S. students were reading the FYS works—for example the Greek classics—in translation, he suggested that we allow the Chinese students to read them in Chinese. He pointed out that the FYS course was about thinking, not about learning English; while the Chinese students would certainly need to improve their English, they should have the experience, as early as possible in their time at Bard, of engaging with the ideas of the great works.

We happened to have on campus that year, as a visiting professor of history from Sun Yat Sen University in Guangzhou, a faculty member, Maybo Ching, whose Ph.D. was from Oxford University and who was able to teach a Chinese language section of FYS. Translations of the FYS works into Chinese were readily available, both traditional and simplified characters. The arrangement had the additional advantage that the new group of first-year Exception Admit students from China could enter FYS at once, instead of waiting until their second year. It allowed us to learn whether these students were up to the intellectual challenge of college academic work, without having to wait a year.

Some faculty of the College were shocked at this unconventional idea—the "great books" course taught in Mandarin—but the president prevailed. The course has continued to be offered every second year since then, with very good results. Its teachers have moved gradually to the use of English during the school year. This was certainly a key moment in the history of the Conservatory, in which the support and innovative ideas of Leon Botstein not only averted the crisis but also enhanced the daily workings of the Conservatory.

English language proficiency continues to be a challenge in the Conservatory, a necessary challenge because the most gifted students in many parts of the world are encouraged to focus entirely on music, in a feature of the very cultural bias that the Bard Conservatory challenges. We cannot avoid the problem by refusing to admit these students; rather, we need to work with them to make it possible for them to succeed at Bard. Over the years we have increased the intensity of the required ESL course, changing it from 4 to 8 credits. We recently decided that at the end of that course students would need to satisfy a version of Bard's special "admission by essay" criterion before being allowed to register in courses that require a high level of English-language proficiency.

This is perhaps also the place to mention the many success stories involving Conservatory students in the College. Not only have many

Conservatory students turned out to be the among the very strongest in the College in their second majors, but it is frequently observed that Conservatory students are models for other students in the areas of hard work, discipline, ambition, and accomplishment.

Recruitment in Hungary

Beginning with János Sutyák, a trombone player who came to Bard from a village near Debrecen in the fall of 2006, the number of Hungarian students in the Conservatory rose to 18 by 2012. This was due in large part to the extraordinary effort and genius of Olivia Cariño. The story of Olivia and her husband, László Z. Bitó, Bard Class of 1960, needs to be told here. Their role in the Conservatory was transformative.

The story begins in December 1956, after the suppression of the Hungarian uprising by Soviet tanks and troops, when László and a group of approximately three hundred Hungarian "Freedom Fighters" were invited to Bard College for a month of language study and orientation to the United States. At the end of that period, László and his fellow Hungarians delivered a proclamation expressing appreciation to the members of the Bard community "for the tremendous efforts exerted . . . to orient themselves to us Hungarian students." They conferred the title of "Honorary Hungarian College Professor" on the Bard faculty "who thought they could teach us the English language."

László stayed on at Bard and graduated with a degree in biology in 1960. He earned his doctorate at Columbia in cell biology and biophysics, carried out research in London and again at Columbia, and rose through the ranks at Columbia to become professor of ocular physiology. He published more than 150 scientific articles, numerous reviews, and several scientific monographs. In 1994, at the age of 60, László published his first novel. Since then, in addition to acquiring patents for Xalatan, the eye-pressure-lowering glaucoma drug, he has gone on to publish eight more novels and five collections of essays.

In January 2007 Bard held a three-day conference and 50th reunion for the Hungarians who came to Bard in 1956. I met László and Olivia on the day before the opening of the conference in the midst of a fierce snowstorm. They agreed to hike through the snow to the music building to meet János Sutyák and to hear a sample of the playing of some of the Conservatory students.

Our relationship developed from there. When Olivia learned that my next trip to Budapest for auditions for the fall of 2007 admission had gone badly (in fact, no one showed up, because of miscommunication), she took over the organization of the auditions. This included a concert in Budapest of current Conservatory students, a preconcert interview in a Budapest newspaper, a postconcert reception for members of the music community and the diplomatic corps, and well-publicized auditions, this time attended by some 40 applicants.

In each subsequent year Olivia refined and improved the process, meeting with students in advance, helping in the preparation of audition materials, even finding Budapest-based Bard graduates to help Hungarian applicants prepare their application essays. In the meantime, the Bitós made a leadership gift toward matching our challenge grant from the Mellon Foundation, gave scholarship gifts for Hungarian students, and launched the Hungarian Visiting Fellows Program that for three years brought us scores of musicians, ranging from short-term visits from pianists Várjon Dénes and Izabella Simon, violist Peter Barsony, cellist István Varga, and flutist Gergy Ittzés, to semester-long visits from then-students cellist Tamás Zétényi, violist David Toth, and bassist Bence Botar. The Bitós even purchased a contrabassoon in Budapest and paid for its seat on an airplane so that David Nagy, our bassoon student, could bring it to Bard. The story continues below.

Vocal Arts Program

In February 2004, before the Conservatory, opened, I wrote to the soprano Dawn Upshaw to ask whether she would consider becoming involved, in any capacity. I had met her years before, after a concert she gave with Richard Goode at UCLA. I knew she was a great artist and I had heard wonderful things from many of my friends about her as a teacher and as a person. Dawn suggested that we meet to talk—it turned out that she received my letter around the same time that she had begun to think about the possibility of teaching.

Our conversation led to a meeting at Bard with Leon Botstein, in which we asked Dawn to assume the leadership of the vocal program in the Conservatory—either undergraduate or graduate, her choice. Dawn preferred the idea of creating a small graduate program. We agreed to meet throughout that academic year, 2005–06, to plan the program, and that the first students would be admitted in the fall of 2006. Those meetings, which included Melvin Chen and Carol Yaple (Dawn's good friend and publicist), were exciting and productive, as Dawn thought through a program with a focus on art song, connections with text, and work with theater directors. It also included movement specialists and personalized career building in addition to the more customary parts of a vocal arts program (such as voice lessons and diction). Voice teachers were interviewed and hired, promotional materials drafted and designed, and recruiting began in earnest.

It became clear early on that an associate director was needed, partly because of Dawn's busy performance schedule, and a prime candidate emerged: pianist and vocal coach Kayo Iwama, Dawn's longtime associate in the Tanglewood summer voice program. Kayo and her husband, Frank Corliss, left Boston to join Bard. Frank created and administers the Postgraduate Collaborative Piano Fellowship and serves now as associate director of the Conservatory. He and Kayo were on campus for the opening of the program, along with our first eight vocal arts graduate students, in September 2006.

Enrollment Growth

The Conservatory has grown from 21 (in 2005) to 136 students, including undergraduates, certificate students, vocal arts students, and conducting students. In 2009 we received permission from the New York State Education Department to offer the certificate in Advanced Performance Studies (APS). That category has proven useful in cases where we were not satisfied with the pool of undergraduate applicants for particular instruments and were able to add highly qualified graduate students for two-year certificate programs of study. These APS graduate students participate fully in the instrumental studios, the orchestra, and the chamber music program of the Conservatory.[1] Beginning in the fall of 2006 we added eight students in the Graduate Vocal Arts Program, and another eight the following year. We have not always reached the target number of 16 students for this program; as of this writing, however, 18 vocal arts students are enrolled. Enrollment in the Graduate Conducting Program (Orchestral and Conducting tracks) has fluctuated around 10; there are now 11 conducting students in the Conservatory.

So far in our first nine years of operation, 63 undergraduate students have completed the B. Music–B.A. program and graduated with the two degrees.[2]

We are nearly at full strength. I estimate an increase of 14 students over the next five years, adding strength in violin, bass, and a few wind instruments, bringing the total enrollment of the Conservatory to 150.

In 2004, as plans for opening the Conservatory became definite, some last-minute modifications were made to the renovation of the Edith C. Blum Institue, home of the Music Program. A seminar room was redesigned as an office for the Conservatory director, and some office space was assigned to the Conservatory. Beyond that, Melvin Chen had a piano studio in Blum. When the Graduate Vocal Arts Program opened, the Ward Manor Gatehouse, previously the site of two small faculty apartments, was given over to the use of that program.

That was the situation for the first seven years of the Conservatory, even as it doubled and tripled in size—the Vocal Arts Program was separated from the rest of the Conservatory, which itself shared space with the Music Program of the College. Master classes and graduation recitals were held in Olin Auditorium, a hall of 370 seats in the center of campus, or in Blum Hall or Bard Hall, performance spaces with a capacity of about 50.

In the spring of 2009 Leon Botstein returned from a trip to Budapest with the exciting news that László Bitó had offered to help the Conservatory with its space problem. Throughout the summer of 2010 I worked with the campus architect, Robert Nilsson, on ideas for a new Conservatory wing of the existing Blum Institute building. In October Debra Pemstein, Bard's vice president for development and alumni/ae affairs, and I made a presentation to the Bitós in Budapest, using a photo album on the history of the Conservatory since 2005 and a set of schematic architectural drawings and cost estimates for a possible new wing. László had a number of questions and ideas, and we agreed to pursue these, with cost options. In the next days I held auditions in Budapest, and on the day I left Olivia sent me an e-mail, thanking us for sharing our plans and saying there was "still much homework left to do."

By early December 2010, I was able to answer László's questions, with cost estimates. Olivia replied that they would call me in a few days, after their meeting with Leon in Budapest. On the morning of December 10,

I received Leon's report of the meeting at which the Bitós agreed to a gift of $9.2 million for construction of the new Conservatory home. As I wrote to Olivia and László, I was thrilled beyond words, and filled with gratitude and excitement.

Things moved quickly. In January 2011, the Bard trustees approved the construction of the building by Deborah Berke Partners, with a start date in September 2011 and completion by December 2012. A ground-breaking ceremony took place on October 28, 2011, during Bard's Family Weekend. We moved into the new space on schedule in January 2013, finally bringing together the Graduate Vocal Arts Program with the rest of the Conservatory.

The formal opening, attended by the Bitós, the architect, and many other guests, took place on April 8, 2013. It included the reading of a celebratory poem by Robert Kelly and a performance of a Bach work for chorus and instruments. The building includes 15 teaching studios, a main office, an elegant lobby, and a beautiful performance space. The rooms have marvelous acoustics; halls and rooms are filled with light. Like the Bitós themselves, the building's effect on the Conservatory is transformative.

The Orchestra Program

In the first years of the Conservatory, a chamber orchestra was assembled twice each semester, with rehearsals clustered before a concert. Only later, as our numbers increased, and when Leon Botstein became music director of the orchestra and Erica Kiesewetter joined us as director of orchestral studies, did the orchestra become a regular program with twice-weekly rehearsals and four main programs each year. Leon generally conducts two of the concerts; guest conductors have included Fabio Machetti, Harold Farberman, Xian Zhang, Michael Gilbert, Guillermo Figueroa, Nanse Gum, David Alan Miller, Gisele Ben-Dor, Rossen Milanov, Marcelo Lehninger, and Cristian Maceleru.

Since October 2010 the orchestra has performed every year at Eastern Correctional Facility in Napanoch, New York, a maximum-security prison. This was first arranged in May 2010 when I attended a graduation ceremony for the Bard Prison Initiative at Eastern, and we saw that the auditorium would be suitable for a concert. It was arranged for the following fall. The orchestra manager, Fu-chen Chan, had to make an advance trip with Max Kenner, head of the Bard Prison Initiative; as I recall, she took along a cello as a sample of an instrument that would have to pass through the security check.

For the concert, we brought two busloads of students, preceded by a truck with timpani, harp, other percussion instruments, and 90 music stands. The students were nervous and excited as they arrived for the preconcert rehearsal. Cell phones, wallets, keys—everything—had to be left in the bus. Each student and guest went through an elaborate check-in and metal-detector scan, and received a fluorescent mark on the wrist. When the halls were cleared of inmates we were escorted to the auditorium. The room had a metallic, dry acoustic, not unlike many high school auditoriums. The orchestra squeezed onto the stage, basses and percussion hardly visible at the back edges.

The inmates filed into seats at the back and middle of the auditorium, for the concert, leaving a gap of about fifteen rows behind the guests in the front six or eight rows. The students wore concert clothes—men in tuxedos, women in black dresses. The program began with words of introduction by the prison superintendent, followed by greetings and explanatory comments by Leon Botstein on the pieces to be played. The students played with intensity. The fans in the room had been turned off to reduce the noise, and as the heat rose, the students' faces glowed with perspiration. The applause after each piece was thunderous. They played three works—a Rossini overture, the Ferdinand David Trombone Concerto, and a Dvořák symphony. When the concert ended, Leon took questions from the inmates. Each questioner began with words of appreciation for the performance. How were the pieces selected? How did students come to choose the instruments they played? How was it different to play in a prison? One inmate asked, where would his children be able to hear this kind of music?

The prison concert has turned out to be a much-anticipated annual event. Several years after her graduation from Bard, one of our students, a violinist who went on to postgraduate study at Curtis, told me, in the midst of negative comments about her recent concert experience at a prestigious summer festival, that the most satisfying concert experiences she had ever had were the prison concerts during her years at Bard.

In May 2010, to celebrate the Conservatory's fifth birthday, the orchestra played in Alice Tully Hall in New York's Lincoln Center. Chen was soloist in George Perle's second piano concerto, and Dawn Upshaw soloed in the Fourth Symphony of Mahler. To bring the orchestra to full size we included a substantial number of ringers, as we also did for rehearsals and concerts throughout the year. In a favorable review in the New York *Times*, the critic felt called upon to note the number—even, as I recall, the exact count—of the nonstudents in the orchestra.

In each subsequent year the number of ringers has decreased. In 2011 the orchestra played at Sanders Theater at Harvard University. In June 2012 it made a three-week tour of greater China, and in May 2013 returned to Alice Tully Hall. In June 2014 the orchestra performed in eight cities of Eastern Europe and Russia.

The Chamber Music Program

Melvin Chen and I placed considerable importance on developing a strong chamber music program in the Conservatory. Structural factors make this somewhat difficult: the groups generally change from semester to semester, rehearsals are scheduled by the groups themselves, and no group performances and tours build morale, like that of an orchestra or a chorus. In my own conservatory experience, chamber music was secondary in the curriculum—rehearsals and coaching sessions were rescheduled or cancelled to make room for other priorities.

At Bard, we have tried to meet these difficulties in several ways: we require chamber music in every semester for every student, we organize frequent chamber music master classes by visiting artists to raise the visibility of the program, we provided funds on several occasions to support participation in the finals of national chamber music competitions, and, perhaps most important, we organize many outside performance opportunities for mixed groups of faculty and students playing together.

We adopted a policy that all groups would have a performance opportunity toward the end of each semester, but that for the outside engagements of the mixed groups, the choice of players would be "non-democratic," based entirely on the student's level of playing. One student quartet that formed during the Conservatory's first year stayed together for five years, survived a few changes in personnel, called itself the Chimeng Quartet (from "Qimeng," the Chinese word for "enlightenment," a major theme of the First-Year Seminar), and achieved considerable success, including an invitation to perform at the Shanghai World Expo in 2010 and winning the Silver Medal at the Fischoff Chamber Music Competition. The Chimeng Quartet received considerable publicity, including a front-page profile in the U.S. edition of *China Daily*. Another student group, the Hudson Valley Brass Quintet, capped off a successful performance season with two weeks as an invited ensemble at the Stellenbosch Chamber Music Festival in South Africa.

The cumulative effect of these activities has been as hoped, a strong presence of chamber music in the life of the Conservatory. Many groups stay together from semester to semester. A marathon concert starting at 1 p.m., with a break for supper (with the audience) and continuing late into the evening, is needed at the end of each semester to accommodate the performances of that semester's ensembles.

Fund-raising

In 2005 the Conservatory received an Implementation Grant of $230,000 (divided over three years) from The Andrew W. Mellon Foundation—a follow-up to the $40,000 Planning Grant of 2004. In 2008 the Conservatory was invited to submit a proposal for an endowment challenge grant, restricted to support of the "core undergraduate academic program." As part of the Mellon's consideration of that proposal, we were asked to confirm that we would not depart from our commitment to the double-degree requirement, and that we would strive to enroll more U.S. students. I believe this second point was based on the view at the Foundation that U.S. students would in general be better prepared for the academic part of the double-degree program; perhaps they were also concerned that the difficulties described above in connection with the English-language proficiency of the international students might impede or even sink the double-degree program. We made both commitments.

I was also asked, during consideration of our proposal, what level of matching funds we could commit to. It was clear in this connection that at least a 1:1 match would be required, and that agreement to a match beyond 1:1 would be welcomed and would strengthen our proposal. In my enthusiasm (and naiveté?) I agreed to a match as high as 3:1— that we would raise $3 for every $1 from the Foundation. In 2008 we were awarded a $2.5 million grant to be used as an endowment for the Conservatory's core undergraduate academic program (not to be used for financial aid) on condition that we raise three times that amount, i.e., $7.5 million within four years.[3]

Due to the 2008 downturn of the economy, we were unable to make the first deadline (September 2012) for raising those matching funds—we had raised approximately $2 million by that time. We requested and were granted a four-year deadline, to September 2016. At the time of this writing, we have raised $3.2 million toward the match. I hope we may cap our celebration of the Conservatory's 10th year by reaching the $7.5 million goal.

Our Conservatory remains a work in progress, so this brief history ends with a few simple reflections, no grand conclusion.

The arrival of each new student brings the excitement of a promise to be kept. Each graduation recital reveals a miracle of growth. Each master class, orchestra performance, and chamber music concert brings pride and, to be honest, a certain incredulousness that our Conservatory is as real and successful as it has become. Each day spent with our amazing staff fills me with admiration and gratitude for the hard work accomplished so well, with dedication and, above all, with love for our students.

NOTES

1. Total of undergraduates and APS students by year: Fall 2005: 21; Fall 2006: 36; Fall 2007: 53; Fall 2008: 55; Fall 2009: 73; Fall 2010: 85; Fall 2011: 90; Fall 2012: 92; Fall 2013: 98; Fall 2014: 107.

2. Total of graduates of the undergraduate double-degree program: 2008: 1; 2009: 1; 2010: 10; 2011: 15; 2012: 12; 2013: 9; 2014: 15. The first two graduates had transferred to Bard from other conservatories.

3. The $2.5 million was transferred to the College with the understanding that as increments of $100,000 (cash, not pledges) were placed in a Conservatory endowment fund, $33,333 of Mellon Foundation funds would also be added to that endowment fund, and the interest on those combined endowment funds would be available to the Conservatory.

On the Education of Musicians: A Manifesto[1]

ROBERT MARTIN

Aristotle wrote that young people would profit from the study of music but should give it up well before the point of becoming professionals. He agreed with Plato that music brings harmony to the souls of the young, but he drew a clear line between well-bred gentlemen and professional musicians.

> The right measure will be obtained if students of music stop short of the arts which are practiced in professional contests . . . for in this the performer practices the art, not for the sake of his own improvement, but in order to give pleasure, and that of a vulgar sort, to his hearers. For this reason, the execution of such music is not the part of a freeman but of a paid performer . . . *Politics* 8-6 (in the Jowett translation).

This is a class prejudice. Musicians, actors, jugglers, comics, and other entertainers have been treated throughout history essentially as servants, not as fellow citizens. Joseph Haydn is a prime example, responsible not only for composing and performing for the prince and his guests, but also for the laundry of the court musicians. A first-class education, historically, was deemed appropriate for those who would assume leadership positions in society, not for the working classes and not for the entertaainers (and incidentally, not for women, although that gradually changed). It is striking that the founding of the first great modern conservatory in the western world, that of Paris in 1795, was a socially progressive, forward-looking attempt to bring dignity to the profession. It was felt that those who would play in the theaters and concert halls should be not only adept at the instrument but also grounded in aural skills, solfeggio, and music history. This was a big step forward from the time of the very first conservatories in the West, in the fourteenth century, when orphans in the

Italian *ospedale* were trained to play and sing in public to solicit charity for their food and lodging.

The education received at the Paris Conservatory in no way matched that received by the children of the upper classes, however, because it was restricted almost entirely to music. Amazingly little has changed since then. Randall Thompson put it quite simply in 1967: "The direction of a conservatory is frankly vocational. That of a liberal arts college is not. The aim of a liberal arts college is to produce integrated citizens."[2]

I think it is time to realize that young musicians not only need, but also deserve, a first-class education in the liberal arts and sciences.

It is tempting to come to a very different conclusion. Consider the familiar distinction between broad general education and specialized training in a particular field. We all recognize that highly skilled vocations such as carpentry or plumbing or surgery require intense, specialized training and apprenticeship. Music does also. Indeed, the length and intensity of training needed for a career as a pianist or violinist exceeds that of these other examples. So why should a budding musician waste time with a liberal arts[3] education? That is the first question I will try to answer here, by arguing that *a liberal arts education is not only valuable but also crucial in the education of young musicians*. After that I will try to answer a second question: Where does the idea come from that gifted young musicians should focus exclusively, or almost exclusively, on music?

My argument for the necessity, not just the desirability, of a liberal arts education has three parts. The first two parts present important though not ultimately decisive considerations in support of this claim, but the third part presents a consideration that I think is indeed decisive.

1. Other things being equal, the life of a musician with a solid general education will be richer and happier than that of one without it. I suppose this is hardly controversial, yet it is important nonetheless. All the parts of a liberal arts education—the single courses taken as part of the exploratory phase of one's education, or the in-depth study that constitutes a "major"—will in later years become a sources of pleasure and edification. Not coincidentally, the broad education will connect one to other interesting people at many stages of one's life.

2. A liberal arts education provides a career advantage in music. The ease and self-confidence in writing and speaking that comes from a liberal arts education help a musician in a wide variety of practical ways, from preconcert talks and the preparation of program materials to negotiations with employers and funders. Further, one need only think of YoYo Ma's *Silk Road* project, for example, to see the power of a career-enhancing idea born of knowledge of history and the imagination to ask penetrating questions. This is a point of broad applicability. Who could suppose that the success of individuals such as Steve Jobs and Mark Zuckerberg came simply or even mainly from their facility with algorithms? Even without finishing a liberal arts college education, both developed the broad and far-ranging skills and habits of mind characteristic of liberal arts education that served them well as innovators and leaders.

3. A liberal arts education will make a musician a *better* musician, adding refinement, discrimination, and imagination to technical prowess. This is the part of the argument most in need of justification. Points (1) and (2) are important but not decisive. One could grant that a liberal arts education brings pleasure and career advantages, yet argue that, when it comes to the music itself, it is the years of practice, study with master teachers, and performance experience, on top of the essential ingredient of musical talent—not a liberal arts education—that determines the quality of the outcome. Indeed, some would argue that it is the *willingness to sacrifice* a great deal—including the personal and career advantages of a liberal arts education—that characterizes the most dedicated musicians, that allows them, through single-minded focus, to become great musicians.

I think this is wrong, and I will try to show it is wrong. I will argue that the skills and attitudes fostered by an education in the liberal arts and sciences are exactly those that will make the difference between technical excellence and genuine artistry.

What kind of argument is possible here? I have to assume that the reader recognizes the difference between technical excellence and genuine artistry. We have all heard performances that are frustrating because they are, in a sense, faultless, but still unaffecting and uninteresting. The performance may be well in tune and rhythmically solid, with pleasing sound and generally "musical" phrasing, good tempo, and ample energy. There are no "mistakes," yet our minds wander. By contrast, a performance of authentic artistry holds our attention. We recognize a palpable sense of concentration and of overall direction among the parts of the piece, either toward what is coming or reflective of what has been heard; there is a sense of freshness and discovery, as though the performer is inventing the piece; there is moment-to-moment characterization of musical materials, expressive of wit, drama, pathos, longing, grandeur, and mystery; and there is even more—all quite difficult to characterize in words but conspicuous in performance.

Who is to say where artistry comes from? We speak of musical talent, and anyone who has worked with young musicians for many years knows how important but also elusive that concept is. I have argued elsewhere[4] that at least part of musical talent is responsiveness to the "stuff" of music: rhythms, chord progressions, textures, timbres, silences, and the other things out of which musical works are constructed. But talent alone does not produce artistry. Artistry is exquisitely sensitive to the details of particular works. *The qualities strengthened by a liberal arts education include those that conduce toward the grasp of such details, and therefore toward artistry.* These are the qualities of curiosity, intellectual adventurousness, the ability to see connections, and the mental discipline to focus on complex arguments and narratives. The day may come when we know enough about the human brain to quantify these neurological connections: how the study of mathematics can affect the performance of a Schubert piano sonata, or how the study of a foreign language and culture can affect the performance of a Bach suite. But even now we can recognize the result and know that it is real.

Let me give a more specific example of the ways that a liberal arts education can improve one's music making. There is an interesting musicological literature on the presence of "topics"—the Greek *topoi*—especially in music of the eighteenth century.[5] The topics are such things as the hunt, the church, the courtly dance, the forest, the village wedding. Musical references to these topics are present even in so-called absolute music—for example, a fragment of a horn call representing the hunt, or a modal chord progression representing church worship. These allusions were and remain recognizable (almost unconsciously) by audiences as such, providing an extra-musical dimension. The result for the listener is a general sense of connection to the concerns of everyday life. What is the significance for the performer? To some extent the performer needs to "bring out" the topics; more important, a broadly educated performer will be likely to have background knowledge of the cultural phenomena represented by the topics. This, at the very least, will likely enhance the performer's concentration. It will communicate itself to the audience as a kind of insight and a source of delight.

One can imagine a number of objections to my claims about the value of a liberal arts education for music making. One objection, surely the one most frequently made, is that that there is simply not enough time for academic studies beyond the demands of the instrument. My experience is that gifted young people generally have more energy than they know what to do with, and that fewer hours of intelligent practice are much better than many hours of mindless practice. Furthermore, the level of technical accomplishment of young players has risen dramatically over the years. It is evident that many students arrive at conservatory needing musical refinement (and all that supports it) far more than hours of technical work.

In truth, I am often surprised by how readily these conclusions are accepted by my fellow musicians and music educators. That leads to the second question: *Where then, does the idea come from, that gifted young musicians should focus exclusively, or almost exclusively, on music?* If this view is as misguided as I claim, what accounts for its stubborn hold?

I think two main factors are at work here. The first, which I have already mentioned, I will call the *Aristotle prejudice*. It is the view, quite simply, that the proper general education of the elite is not necessary or appropriate for the training of entertainers. That view, unfortunately, is alive and well today. Indeed, it is so familiar and ingrained that it is often difficult to recognize.

The Aristotle prejudice should not be confused with the different but related view that vocational topics—for example, journalism, law, accounting, hospitality management, engineering—should not be part of the course of study of liberal arts colleges. One could say broadly that Aristotle disparaged that which is done for material gain, and there is the sense that the best liberal arts education eschews vocational considerations. But, contrary to the Aristotle prejudice, the liberal arts college of today views specialization for the professions simply as a later stage of education, built upon the foundation it provides.

Another factor that contributes to the prevalent view of conservatory education is the nineteenth-century Romantic view of the exalted genius, a person of inspiration, madness, and obsessive focus, a person with a higher calling, in direct touch with a spiritual force. We all recognize this as a central conceit of Romantic literature, poetry, and painting. A famous example is the persona of Beethoven that was constructed in the second half of the nineteenth century. We recognize this notion in the mystique surrounding Franz Liszt and other virtuosi at whose performances audience members were said to faint from excitement. We recognize the philosophical underpinnings of this notion in Schopenhauer's view that music—and only music—provides access to the Will, the world of things in themselves, otherwise entirely hidden from human view. The Romantic conception of music and genius, still very much alive today, teams up with the Aristotle prejudice: *it makes peace with what I regard as the shortchanging of the young musician by glorifying single-mindedness.* This is a potent and insidious combination: gifted musicians are denied access to the education associated with upper-class opportunity, while being assured that the loss is not significant. The Romantic conception makes a virtue of an intellectual deficit!

Of course, there is much of value in the Romantic conception. The Romantics understood that music is not only pleasing but also deep; not only attractive but also important. There is truth in the feeling that high musical attainment is wondrous, even magical. But nothing in Romanticism should keep a young musician of the highest aspirations from having a fine general education. One can be inspired and in touch with the muses *and* profit from a rigorous liberal arts education. Artistry is enhanced by the education.

It is no surprise then that undergraduate students in the Bard College Conservatory of Music are required to pursue *two* degrees over a five-year period: the bachelor of music degree and the bachelor of arts degree in a field other than music. The high success rate of our graduates in gaining admission to the most competitive graduate programs in the United States and abroad has been heartening. More than 90 percent continue in music; a few have chosen to pursue graduate study in other fields, including economics, biochemistry, and information systems.

NOTES

1. An early version of this essay was presented in a panel, "Aspects of the Notion of Artistic Integrity," at the 2012 Annual Congress of the Association Européenne des Conservatoires, Académies de Musique et Musikhochschulen, November 10, 2012. This version owes much to the helpful comments of George Rose.

2. *College Music: An Investigation for the Association of American Colleges,* p. 97.

3. From now on I use the words *liberal arts* in the broad sense, to include the sciences, humanities, and social sciences.

4. "Musical 'Topics' and Expression in Music," *Journal of Aesthetics and Art Criticism* Vol. 53 No. 4 (Autumn 1995), reprinted in this volume.

5. See, for example, Wye Jamison Allanbrook, *Rhythmic Gesture in Mozart* (University of Chicago Press, 1983) and references included there.

Reflections on the Bard Conservatory's Graduate Vocal Arts Program

DAWN UPSHAW

Everything in life (and in art) evolves in order to truly thrive. And in the world of music, the art form of vocal performance is no exception. In fact, the teaching and education offered in support of the growth of this living—literally, "breathing"—art form do not escape this constant requirement and must follow suit: in order for instruction and guidance in this art form to be truly effective and inspiring, it must at every moment be open to new expressive possibilities and must be welcoming of organic transformation—of evolution. Instruction must come by way of openness to and, even, expectation of that which we have never before encountered. At a time when we hear constant rumblings of concern in the broader classical music world ("Is the song recital on its way out?" "Is the accessibility of music through all our electronic devices becoming a substitute for attending live performance?") we find we are blessed with new generations of extremely talented and imaginative young people who are not deterred, who are seeking to better understand (as did we at their ages and as we do still) the impact and power of musical expression, who are eager to contribute in answer to the world's needs, and whose creative passions for music, poetry, theater, and the mysteries and beauty of the human voice engage and teach *us*, and await our response.

In my role as artistic director of the Graduate Vocal Arts Program at the Bard Conservatory, and as an educator, I seek to engage those passions with my own. In fact, the fundamental link between myself and our students—and between myself and my colleagues—is this passion for music and passion for words residing in us, feeding our own imaginations and informing and guiding our engagement with each other and with the world around us. We each have our own histories. Whether these students have come to our program from other conservatory programs, from a liberal arts undergraduate education, from a rich choral background, whether they have developed a love for chamber music or have had extensive exposure to opera, they have found, some place along the way and over their singular history, a sense of identity and expression through their music making. And to one degree or another, they are very conscientiously investigating the idea that the act itself of making music may be an essential part of who they are, who they hope to be, and a vehicle through which they might contribute meaningfully to the world, to "say" what they need and want to "say" while living on this planet.

This has certainly been true for me. My early experience, singing and performing the music and words of Pete Seeger, Bob Dylan, and Peter, Paul, and Mary in schools and churches with my parents and my older sister during the civil rights movement of the 1960s, left me with an introductory sense of the great power of music to move, to awaken, and to connect with and bring together large and small gatherings of people around common human experiences of yearning, loss, resolve, and celebration. Over time, and through a variety of other kinds of musical experiences and through the influence of other remarkable artists and mentors, that sense has naturally deepened. But I think now of those earliest years as an important seedbed of my own desire and need to sing, and of the beginning of my own developing discovery of the meaning, joy, and sense of generous giving that can come through performance.

Each of our vocal students carries within her / himself unique seedbeds, and whatever those seedbeds have been in their lives, as an educator I want to nurture something in the developmental and explorative process that our vocal program provides that might take those earlier influences into account and yield opportunities for our students for continued growth in self-discovery and in confidence. I also want us to focus long and hard on providing the highest quality of instruction we can, and to offer exposure to the all-important fundamentals of artful singing: understanding and application of good vocal technique; honoring and honing the skills necessary to build good musicianship; appreciation for the power of words; appreciation for and ability to use expressive diction; attention to freedom and release of breath; learning the importance of being comfortable in one's own body and appreciating the great potential in the expressivity of movement; study in foreign language; development of acting skills; and study of and appreciation for the historical context of particular works.

But as a teacher, above all else I want to keep my eyes on *this* prize for our students: How does one continue to seek honesty, openness, and generous expression and conveyance through music performance?

This is, of course, a very personal issue, and not one to be directed or controlled by someone else's instructions, guidelines, or specified rules. It is, rather, a private journey, a continuous process of genuine "seeking" over time. When I was first approached by Bard College president Leon Botstein and by Robert Martin, director of the Bard Conservatory, they asked me if I would be interested in leading and building a Conservatory voice program for undergraduates. I knew already that I was most intrigued by my teaching experiences with a slightly older age group—a slightly more advanced skill level—through my work with graduate-level singers. This is the time in a young singer's life—anywhere from the early to late 20s—that I find especially rich with possibility, "on the verge" of a marked, deeper maturity and understanding both emotionally and intellectually, therefore on the cusp of truly understanding what it is they are attempting to do, with a greater awareness as well of the responsibilities this path entails. As an educator, I find this a fascinating moment to become engaged in the life of a singer.

I was very impressed with President Botstein and Robert Martin's eagerness to shift toward this idea, toward creating a master's degree program. In addition to creating a program that could focus on the needs of this particular level of development, it was also very important to me that our Graduate Vocal Arts Program be intimate (with a total number of participants at any given time of just sixteen to twenty students), enabling all the faculty to work deeply and personally with every single student and with each other, as we attempt to guide most effectively each of these uniquely talented individuals, each with their unique offerings, strengths, and weaknesses.

Inasmuch as our two-year program constitutes but a dot on the timeline of our students' lives, it has been my goal as director of this program that I and our faculty work as imaginatively and closely as possible to create a curriculum that has the potential to facilitate the personal evolution of each young singing artist during his / her brief but potent time with us. I know from my personal performing experience, and from my observations as a music educator, that a young performing musician grows exponentially, becomes intimately familiar with her or his own unique artistry, and excels most intensely through performance itself, and through the process of the preparation leading into that performance. As singing artists, we carry ourselves forward in the most productive, engaged, and enthusiastic way when we are exploring and collaborating with other inspired artists to reach the goal of truthful conveyance. I am excited to collaborate with other faculty and with our students, tapping into our imaginations as we create and prepare together these very important performance opportunities.

My goal for this intimate Vocal Arts Program (and, as I write on this date in the beginning of 2015, we are already well on our way) is to continue enhancing this curriculum, which can be centered around our Core Seminar courses each semester, culminating in performances on campus and also within the surrounding Mid-Hudson Valley communities, providing a haven and a platform for our students' exploration and expression. There is such an obvious double benefit in this: engaging the Bard community with meaningful musical experiences, and simultaneously providing our graduate vocal arts students with performance opportunities that can enrich and expand their experience of the generosity—the offering up and sharing of the gift—that performance can be.

Dismantling VCRs:
How the Familiar Can Inspire

RYLAN GAJEK-LEONARD

I. Before Bard

Early Interests

My interest in non-musical subjects arose quite late. Until 11th grade, I was a student at Gulf Islands Secondary School on Salt Spring Island, British Columbia, Canada, where my teachers supported my extra-curricular endeavors: playing chamber music, taking theory classes at the Victoria Conservatory of Music, and performing with the Greater Victoria Youth Orchestra. These undertakings required weekly Monday afternoon ferry commutes. Additional school days were cut short so that I could participate in master classes. Although I was a good student, it seemed necessary to minimize academic responsibilities so that I could focus more on music. I withdrew from French Immersion, which I had pursued for six years. School advisors dissuaded me from taking the more difficult science courses, and I avoided mathematics throughout 9th and 10th grades.

This initial aversion to mathematics resulted in my having to take four math courses back-to-back through 11th and 12th grades. In order to solve homework problems, I was forced to review basic material. This review and the quick succession of courses helped me trace new material back to its roots and see its purpose. I found satisfaction in understanding not only the answer to a problem, but also why it turned out that way and why we were studying it. When I was not practicing my music in the science room during lunch hour, I Googled unsolved math problems and properties of the infamous "imaginary unit" (the square root of negative one) on library computers.

Before the start of 12th grade, I moved to Calgary, Alberta, invited by the cello pedagogue John Kadz to participate in a new advanced performance program through Mount Royal University. The cello class consisted of four students in addition to myself: another high school student, a graduate of McGill University, a transfer student from McGill University, and a graduate of the University of Calgary. The program was intense: weekly studio class, twice-weekly lessons, two solo recitals, and a chamber recital per year. I lived at the university with two other students in a town house, working to complete my 12th-grade course requirements through a distance-learning program in British Columbia.

I first heard of the Bard College Conservatory of Music through John Kadz. A student of his had auditioned at Bard, drawn to the well-known faculty, and he suggested Bard as a possible fit for me because of my growing interest in academics. After some Internet research and due consideration, I submitted an application.

As a child, I spent time dismantling videocassette recorders (VCRs): snipping and twirling wires, gluing this little wheel to that motor, soldering some lights to a green circuit board and plugging it all back in to see what happened. Usually, nothing. Occasionally, some whirring and flashing, or smoking and smoldering. For this reason, trips to the landfill became a particular joy. Upon leaving the dump, the car trunk would be scattered with various illegitimately acquired "treasures."

I came to realize that something that seemed familiar could be made mysterious by tweaking it, just a bit. I knew how to work a VCR and the purpose it served, but I did not know what made it a VCR. Gutting it let me see it. Exploration became the goal.

Music and mathematics began to function similarly to VCRs. They concealed secrets. I was frustrated and amazed with the cello because I knew that it could sound good—I had heard my teacher play—and I knew that it made me feel a certain way, but I did not know why or how. Early practicing was a time for learning the mechanics of playing: where to place my fingers, how to hold the bow, which physical movements made what sounds. I did not know what would become of it, but I enjoyed the feeling of playing and liked to see what the instrument could do under my control.

Mathematics was similar. I encountered it while mildly interested in it and with only the tools of basic arithmetic. More time spent with the subject made operations more familiar, but I was left mystified when these operations were manipulated to surprise me, such as solving a previously unsolvable equation, $x^2+1=0$, by plugging in the imaginary unit, $x=\sqrt{-1}$.

I began to sense a beauty that—in twelve short months—would seduce me into pursuing a double degree.

While considering the choice to pursue a double major, I had reservations. The response from my family and mentors was basically positive. Most family members encouraged the option: if music did not work out, then I would have a "backup" profession. My professors supported the idea because of my interest in school subjects. If I could juggle schoolwork and practice time, there would be no problem.

Some of my peers were less enthusiastic. By pursuing a second degree, they said, I would be missing opportunities and musical growth. It seemed simple: time spent away from music is time lost toward music; squandered practice can only result in sub-par musicians; following one interest would take away from the other. I began to wonder: Would I graduate from college only to achieve mediocrity in two fields?

Visiting Bard

Four of us were led into a small room with light-blue painted brick arches and neon tube lights. I could hear printers shuffling in the distance.

"These are Senior Projects," our guide said, gesturing lazily toward the shelf upon shelf of manuscripts bound in black leather. The books dominated the space, sitting tightly packed on metal shelves, each shelf equipped with a circular wheel that allowed the volumes to be shifted against each other for storage.

It was early February 2011. I had flown to New York from Calgary, Alberta, after being invited to perform a live audition at the Bard College Conservatory of Music. My mother and I were standing under the low ceilings on the first floor of the Stevenson Library, ogling the books with our heads tipped slightly to the right as we tried to make out the shiny, gold-imprinted words on the spines. Some volumes were worn and tattered, others glossy and stiff.

Following the campus tour, my mother and I walked over the soggy entrance mats of Kline Commons, Bard's student dining hall. I wove through a mass of students in the cafeteria, taking care not to slip on the layer of melted snow and grit. After filling my plate with a medley of lasagna, grilled fish, boiled peas and a slice of pizza, I sought out my generous weekend hosts among the crowd of students.

I found Conservatory director Robert Martin and his wife, Katherine, politely chuckling as they listened to my mother speak. Her mouth was spread in a cartoon-like grin as she described what I could only assume was an embarrassing story of my childhood. I moved nervously toward them to take my seat. Advancing slowly, wishing to avoid the crux of my mother's story, I noticed a scruffy-looking student seated in a chair that was mounted atop a dining table. He was dressed in a white robe and was looking straight ahead to the brick wall on the opposite side of the room. His feet were bare and his face unshaven. I gazed up as I walked by, hoping he would not meet my stare. He didn't. I scurried forward and took my seat.

At the table, Dr. Martin speculated that the mangy man on the table might consider himself an art installation or a social experiment, perhaps as part of his Senior Project. I explained some of my interests and asked about the inception of the double-degree program. Dr. Martin told me of his undergraduate experience as a double-degree student. He spoke of his difficulties in gaining permission to study simultaneously at Haverford College and the Curtis Institute of Music, unsympathetic professors, and the problems of traveling between the separate institutions. The Bard Conservatory, Martin explained, tried to eliminate the kinds difficulties he had encountered when he completed the two degrees.

After dinner, on the eve of my Conservatory audition, I was sifting through a spring course catalogue I had found perched atop a mass of shelved books that lined my room in the Martin's home. I opened the catalogue and fanned the pages, waiting for something to catch my eye. After stopping to read a few course descriptions in the philosophy and biology sections, I flipped to the contents page, intending to find the section on mathematics. Letting the pages slide out from under my right thumb, I carefully watched the page numbers increase until I reached my destination.

MATH 332
ABSTRACT ALGEBRA
An introduction to modern abstract algebraic systems, including groups, rings, fields, and vector spaces. The course will focus on a rigorous treatment of the theory of groups (quotient groups, homomorphisms, isomorphisms) and vector spaces (subspaces, dimension, linear maps). Prerequisites: MATH 261 Proofs and Fundamentals, and MATH 213 Linear Algebra.

Seeing the word *modern* in student mathematics is rare. Being such an old science, the culmination of high school math brings a student only to the latter half of the seventeenth century, when calculus was developed. This course description was beyond my grasp. Utterly foreign. What was an *isomorphism*? A *field*? I did not understand the words, but I wanted to.

My first visit to Bard affirmed my growing interest in learning more than just music. The possibility of a double major felt more real. I had met someone who had succeeded, seen the room full of Senior Projects required of undergraduate students, and gained a feeling of what Bard was all about. It seemed like a place where experimentation was celebrated and abstract ideas appreciated.

Bard was a place, unlike a high school cafeteria, where a student could sit on a dining table while dirty and garbed in robes. The dining room was a medium for artistic expression. The student's actions forced the hall to become something other than what it was. Its role as a familiar place was tweaked by his unforeseen and unusual presence, inciting confusion among the students and myself. The man had turned the dining hall into a gutted VCR. He had my respect.

Back in Calgary, I walked swiftly to the bus stop in sunny, frigid weather. The wind shook my cello case, strapped tightly to my back. I heard a tiny explosion through the hard plastic surrounding my cello, letting me know that a string had come loose at the pegs, a frustratingly common occurrence in the cold, dry Alberta weather. Nearing the bus stop, I received a call from Dr. Martin. He informed me that I had been accepted into the Bard College Conservatory of Music Class of 2016. I thanked him excitedly and skipped with joy, loosening another string.

II. At Bard

At this writing I am in my fourth year at the Bard Conservatory and have begun research for my Senior Project in mathematics. Pursuing the double-degree program has not been easy. Each semester, Conservatory musicians enroll in several academic courses, lessons, chamber music, and orchestra.

Being part of a student body filled with double majors has helped me, however, in two ways. First, I have been inspired to continue my pursuit; if my stand partner could do it, then so could I. Second, I didn't feel that I was losing musical opportunities by pursuing academic goals. Since everyone was juggling both class work and practice, I never had the feeling that I was practicing any less than my colleagues. If I felt overwhelmed or under-practiced, it seemed reasonable to assume that someone else must be more overwhelmed or more under-practiced.

Work and practice became synonymous. Completing classwork meant gaining practice time. Serenity came after handing in a paper or set of proofs and knowing that a few days of undisturbed practice lay ahead.

I am inspired not only by my colleagues' work ethic, but also by their demeanor. Bardians are generally interesting and interested people. During a seven-country Conservatory Orchestra tour in eastern Europe, while sitting fully suited on stage in Vienna, I was told the secret to producing a bigger sound by fellow cellist and philosophy major Stanley Moore: "Imagine that there's a long cord between you and that guy near the back of the hall. When we start playing, watch it vibrate." Returning from a concert at Bard College at Simon's Rock, Rachel Becker (cellist, physics major, and now luthier) and I discussed the parabolic shape of flashlights, acoustic properties of a violin, and special relativity. The classical studies major and trombonist Václav Kalidova, then sporting a full-grown half beard, has relayed to me the great potential of cello-trombone fusion. I am amazed with the ideas, academic pursuits, and performance abilities of my colleagues.

But it cannot be said that the amount of class work does not restrict, in some respects and on some occasions, our progress in instrumental proficiency. After being advised by my mathematics professor to spend between forty to fifty hours on a seven-question, weeklong, Complex Analysis exam, I began to experiment with alternative sleep schedules, hoping to squeeze extra time out of the day. Fitting in practice where I could, I raced to finish the take-home exam and complete a paper for my course in German literature, which, unfortunately, was due the same day as the analysis exam. I fought back tears during my lesson that week, frustrated from lack of preparation and lack of sleep. It was one of several lessons in which I felt unprepared.

While these occasional bouts of not-enough-practice do happen, they do not detract from musical growth. During my first lesson at Bard, Peter Wiley posed the question, "What are you?" I had just finished playing the first two movements of Dvořák's Cello Concerto in B minor and was anxious about his inquiry. My confused and erroneous response was "a cellist." Wiley explained to me then that I was first an artist, then a musician, and last a cellist.

Identifying myself as an artist changed my view of the cello. I saw it for what it was: an instrument. This helped me to understand that music is not just playing the cello. The instrument serves a greater purpose.

Wiley's proposition implied that the artist should influence the cellist and that the physics of playing should be guided by what I sought to share. But sharing involves possessing, and possessing requires an awareness of possession. Thus I tried to practice by observing my feelings, hoping to become aware of the way I heard a piece, and then manipulating my technique to communicate that feeling. An audience would not understand a concept if I did not understand it myself. I learned that physical practice, though essential, was not everything.

Following this realization, I convinced myself that academic work was, in fact, contributing to my artistic growth. I came to believe that learning not-music could influence learning music, however abstractly. Nothing had to be lost permanently for pursuing multiple interests.

The number of performance opportunities has also helped keep my playing on track. During the spring of 2013, I stabbed my endpin forcefully and triumphantly into the stage of Carnegie Hall as I sat down to perform with my string quartet. Upon finishing our last piece, we rose to sparkling applause. It is fitting, though, that the most appreciative and genuine audience I met that year was a very different one.

Later that year, I sat in the Conservatory Orchestra cello section, bowtie slightly askew as I clutched my bow slightly above the strings, hoping I would not drop it. The air was thick and dry. Leon Botstein held his hands forward, perfectly still, the right one gently grasping a frozen baton. The only movement in the auditorium was the rattling of metal fans lining the ceiling. The moment Botstein began to lower his arms, the room erupted. Yells, whistles, clapping, banging, stomping . . . Any object that could make noise was put to use. The Conservatory Orchestra smiled, facing forward and gently bowing, to the standing men of Eastern Correctional Facility, a maximum-security prison in Napanoch, New York.

The audience consisted of inmates who had signed up for the concert, including about forty who were enrolled in the Bard Prison Initiative, a competitive program that offers undergraduate degrees to a select few. Our annual concert at the prison became a highlight for me and for many colleagues. The audience seemed truly to understand the music. Despite the clattering fans, the hall was completely still. The men's attentiveness was immediate and their yearning magnetic. While performing in the prison, I realized that although the orchestra has its roots in nobility, classical music felt at home there.

A week after the fall 2013 concert, we received a thank-you letter from some of the men. They described the experience as "primal, a fundamental interaction that is, in our humble opinion, essential to the nurturance of one's humanity." They wrote us a poem. The first two lines read:

> *You are bird*
> *Eagle and Dove.*

The Bard Conservatory faculty works hard to include students in performances, lectures, and other endeavors. I have had the opportunity to perform Tchaikovsky's *Souvenir de Florence* with faculty Robert Martin, Melvin Chen, Weigang Li, and two other students, at venues in Hong Kong, Shanghai, and Beijing. At the request of composer Joan Tower, I spoke about Beethoven's Sonata in C Major for Piano and Cello, Op. 102, No. 1, before performing it for her class at Bard's Lifetime Learning Institute.

Furthermore, faculty members have adjusted their schedules to work around student conflicts. Luis Garcia-Renart, a fifty-year veteran of Bard, who has, amazingly, avoided the onset of computers, has shifted his schedule in every possible way to accommodate students. Weekends are not only an option but one that he recommends if his weekly schedule is booked. Luis teaches every instrument, literally, from the vantage point of artistic expression. I once called his landline phone, my body in a knot of frustration, asking if he could meet me later that week. I was having difficulty battling tension in the Shostakovich Cello Sonata. The impromptu lesson resulted in Luis's describing to me the experience of playing the Sonata for Shostakovich himself, while Luis was living in Russia as a student of Mstislav Rostropovich. I played the opening phrase of the first movement for him twice, asking whether emphasis should be on the first or the second note. His answer was "yes."

Music now feels so fully ingrained in me that attempting to separate my experiences into the musical and the non-musical seems naive. Nevertheless, the apparently non-musical connections that I have formed, and the experiences that I have shared with people, have greatly influenced my personal growth.

I have sung the Canadian national anthem for some Conservatory friends while sitting cross-legged at night in Moscow's Red Square. Just prior to the 2013 summer intersession, I was lying on a patch of grass outside of Blithewood mansion on the Bard campus with a classical studies major to my left and a computer science / biology joint major to my right. We were drinking cider and waiting for the pizza we had ordered to arrive. More recently, the Red Hook Fire Department visited my suite in response to billowing smoke from oven-roasted cheese residue. The culprit was homemade lasagna, complete with five-hour-simmered bolognese sauce.

Though explicitly less meaningful, these experiences form a sizable portion of my immediate memory. They are the quickest thoughts to arise when I am in need of creative inspiration. I know them best, and they are always at hand.

III. Beyond Bard

I am still considering what route to take after graduation. Possible options include applying for graduate school in cello performance, attempting a Ph.D. in mathematics, participating in cello competitions, taking time off, getting a job . . . the list goes on. I will likely apply for graduate school. Perhaps in cello. Possibly in mathematics. Robert Martin has pointed out that continuing to play cello while pursuing mathematics is likely easier than continuing to study mathematics while pursuing cello.

Either way, I know that it is possible to combine both professions, provided that I navigate carefully. Learning is familiar, and the prospect of continuing it is a good one. That said, fiddling with old electronics has been my passion since childhood. Regardless of whether I decide to pursue music or mathematics, I hope that dismantling VCRs remains my main objective.

My Experience as a
Bard Conservatory Student

ALLEGRA CHAPMAN

I began my Bard education in August 2005 as one of three piano students in the Bard Conservatory's inaugural class. Everyone in that first class at the Conservatory had a unique story—some students transferred into the program or left high school early, and many came from as far away as Beijing, Berlin, and Malaysia.

Why did I choose Bard? The decision came naturally, but at the last minute. In my final year of high school, I followed the standard college application procedures for a student interested in a music major. I recorded an audition tape, dragged myself to standardized tests, and filled out endless applications trying to prove my individuality in five hundred words. By mid-March, I tied up my college applications and was content with my likely options. I had mostly avoided applying to conservatories because I suspected that a traditional undergraduate conservatory education would leave me feeling incomplete. Instead, I had searched for excellent schools with strong music programs and the possibility of a double major.

My suspicion of conservatories originated from two sources: doubt about the principles behind a traditional conservatory education and acknowledgment of my own omnivorous nature. The doubt stemmed from this: as a young piano student making forays into the music world through festivals and competitions, I absorbed the notion that I would have to focus exclusively on practicing to become a professional pianist. The successful young pianist looked to me like a cross between a professional athlete and a skilled tradesman. I imagined my educational future, if I chose a conservatory training, to be a long process of repetitively honing my physical skills while undergoing a medieval guild apprenticeship—learning my craft at the feet of generations of skilled artisans. This image appealed to me in a certain way and I pursued it for some time, but as I grew older, I began to feel that I had chosen a horribly uncomfortable pair of shoes. Something was missing.

This had partly to do with my own tendencies. As I entered high school, I ping-ponged between obsessions—piano held a steady constant, but faced stiff competition from foreign languages, history, literature, and politics. I perennially quested for my calling with teenage solemnity and wrote countless unreadable entries in my diary. One day I would leave a piano lesson feeling that I had glimpsed the meaning of existence, and the next I would dissolve into tears asking my dog existential questions about the life of an artist. By the end of high school, I came to realize one thing at least: a traditional undergraduate conservatory education was not for me.

A few weeks before my audition trip to the East Coast, I walked nervously into a lesson with my beloved piano teacher, John McCarthy. He pointed to his piano—where I saw a glossy brochure with the Bard logo emblazoned on its cover—and said to me, "It's a risk, but this might be it." The next week, I found myself in Manhattan for the first time in my life, headed to the apartment of the Bard Conservatory's associate director, Melvin Chen. Through some combination of my first exposure to a cold New York winter, the suddenness of my Bard application process, the traveling, and who knows what else, I sat down at his piano completely unable to play. I couldn't even find middle C, let alone perform my opening audition piece. I looked up at Melvin expecting him to chastise me for wasting his time or to say, "Thank you very much," and escort me out his door.

Instead, he laughed, had me take a break, and then asked me to play something else. His unexpected reaction jolted me out of my stupor and I was able to complete the audition. In that moment, Melvin cared more about my long-term potential than about my performance. I knew then that Bard was looking for a different kind of student.

In my visit to the Bard campus, I tramped around in knee-deep snow with Robert Martin, talking about my interests and the new Conservatory. His description of the program exceeded what I had hoped to create for myself at a larger university. I would not have to wade through bureaucracy to find the guidance I needed, and I would not have to justify my double major to my professors. During my campus tour, the administration and faculty all expressed such excitement, idealism, and contagious optimism that the possibilities for the program seemed limitless. I believed in the mission, but more than that, I looked at what the Conservatory hoped to become and saw a community in which my creative impulses would be nurtured, trained, and put to work. Once I realized that I was unlikely to find similar support or guidance in another institution, joining the inaugural class of the Bard Conservatory seemed less of a risk.

In fact, attending the new Conservatory program *was* a risk, but one well worth taking. In my first few years at Bard, I reveled in the entrepreneurial spirit that fueled the program. The Bard Conservatory had no precedent—never before had a music conservatory required its students to earn two undergraduate degrees. Being a student in the first few years of the program felt something like being a microbe in a petri dish. Faculty and administration monitored us closely, regularly inspecting our development. We were encouraged to form opinions about the program and to voice them. I felt part of a close community made up of students and faculty who all had a stake in the outcome of the experiment.

At times, I was particularly grateful for the careful observation of faculty and administration. In my first semester, I successfully petitioned to take more than the recommended number of credits, ignoring the counsel of my advisers and disregarding the massive syllabi of each class. In a November lesson, my piano teacher, Jeremy Denk, noticed that I looked unusually thin and tired. He mentioned my bedraggled appearance to a few administration members and they immediately intervened. I discovered my limitations that first semester, but the school's support and guidance meant that I came away with nothing worse than a bruised ego and a few mediocre grades.

I recall having many conversations with skeptics about the Conservatory program. I was asked, "How do you pursue two degrees without sacrificing something musically or academically?" I never knew quite how to answer that question because it missed the point. At times, I had to practice less to focus on an important paper, or delay studying to prepare for a performance. But ultimately, these priority shifts were not sacrifices; the overall shape of my education depended on them. I was not training to become something specific—a pianist, or an administrator for a nonprofit—but to develop the combination of elements that would make up my whole person. This was the undergraduate education I needed. The specialization could (and did) come later.

At the start of every semester, I eagerly anticipated two events: hunting down my semester's sky-high stack of materials at the Bard bookstore, and my first lesson of the semester with my piano teacher, Jeremy had an unerring ability to help me step back and see the big picture—in my playing, my comprehension of musical concepts, and my technique— and somehow I would leave lessons feeling as if this contextualization had explained the rest of my life, too. Perhaps his own double major as an undergraduate or his kaleidoscopic interests made him an ideal mentor for me. I have been blessed with many inspiring teachers, but Jeremy influenced the way I see the world and myself more than any teacher I have ever had.

My academic and musical studies so enriched each other that they relied on one another. I wrote my first long research paper for a history class on medieval Europe. My brilliant professor was a lanky, wild-eyed young wordsmith who talked at alarming speeds and radiated enthusiasm. Students left his classes murmuring wide-eyed to one another, feeling as if they had made contact with some numinous power. He taught me to love research and writing. As I prepared for the culminating paper of his class, I began to perceive connections between my research and my practicing, and to critique my practicing methods. I suddenly saw what years of piano teachers had tried to convey to me: that preparing for performance was not about repeating myself endlessly, trying to produce perfect, reliable delivery. I had to excavate motives, collect information, make connections, and find different ways to record my discoveries. I needed to experiment with ideas and build a network of musical and technical possibilities to access in performance. I would most likely have realized this at some point in my mindless practicing, but the accidental nature of the discovery made it all the more powerful.

I embraced the travel bug twice, first studying Arabic in Fez, Morocco, and then spending a semester in Budapest. Through Bard's program at Central European University and an exchange between the Bard Conservatory and the Liszt Academy of Music, I was able to continue my dual studies while abroad. My boyfriend, Emanuel, a Conservatory cellist, also studied that semester with me in Budapest. Together we studied cello sonatas with a wonderful cello professor at the Liszt Academy.

For a classical musician and student of history, there is no substitute for living abroad. One day, Emanuel and I entered our professor's small studio prepared to work on the Shostakovich Cello Sonata. We played through the first movement as he perched on a stool in the corner, making small sounds in his soft voice. When we finished, he continued to sit for some time and we saw that he was pondering over how to express himself in English. Finally, he stood up and said to us, "It is good that you cannot understand what this music is. But you must try." He began a halting description of his memories from the Soviet era, quietly asking us to imagine the terror that he had experienced. After some time, he ran out of words and began to stomp across the small room, imitating the boots of Soviet soldiers. He advised us to absorb as much history as we could while in Budapest, and we followed his suggestion, traveling all over Central and Eastern Europe.

The semester after I returned from Hungary, I enrolled in Bard's Globalization and International Affairs program in New York City, where I interned at a nongovernmental organization and studied international relations. The program gave me an invaluable window onto a possible career path. That semester ended before I realized it had begun; I was almost too busy to eat and reached new realms of efficiency in my academic work and practicing.

After a full year away from the Bard campus, I returned to the haven on the Hudson, longing for my stacks of books and secluded practicing. I gleefully sat for hours on my bed, alternately watching the light over the Catskills and devouring essays about deconstructing, complicating, and interrogating. I binged on academic language and practiced obsessively. Perhaps I was avoiding my imminent decision; I knew that the time had come to decide my next step. While driving Jeremy to the local train station, I attempted to corner him with an impossible question: "Could I have a successful career as a pianist?" I should have known better than to ask him to play fortune-teller. He gave me a look that was somehow both sympathetic and profoundly frustrated, answering the only way he could have: "You will never know unless you try."

The following year, I embarked on a daunting mission: to simultaneously write my Senior Project and audition for graduate programs in music. In the winter, I battled blizzards en route to auditions, and in the spring I spent days at my desk, writing hundreds of pages while I amused myself by watching the groundhogs emerge from the snow.

Two conversations guided me. The first took place in a small room bursting with books. I had researched my topic for months, hoarded facts and quotations, and invented far more organizational systems than I could possibly use. And I had fallen behind on my goals; in fact, I had only produced three nonsensical paragraphs. Cecile, my patient adviser, looked at my crazed scribblings and diagrams and said, with a deep sigh, "You know, Allegra, at some point you just have to start writing."

Her words recalled another conversation I had with Jeremy earlier that year after playing a careful and proper run-through of an audition piece. I thought that I had acquitted myself well and turned to him for comments. To my dismay, he leapt from his chair, his hands wildly gesturing in familiar patterns. "Why are you such a good student? Are even your dreams organized? You are an artist now and you have to start acting like one." I was horrified by Jeremy's tirade. Organized dreams seemed to me like the anathema of artistry. Clearly, he thought I was a goody-two-shoes automaton.

Over the years, I have come to see that Jeremy and Cecile's frustrations stemmed from my refusal to leave the student nest. I wanted their reassurance every step of the way. When I should have been looking to my imagination for expressive possibilities or constructing a thesis from my own observations, I clung desperately to teacherly instructions and research. At times, I still find myself in this trap, over-thinking projects or trying to control my playing, and longing for authoritative guidance. Then I think back to my final year at Bard and remember that the most important lesson of my undergraduate education was in trusting myself.

After Bard, I attended The Juilliard School for my master's degree. The transition to a traditional conservatory was not easy for me, but eventually I cherished my time there. I viewed it as a chance to polish my technical skills and to truly specialize in performance. It might seem backward to develop the intangible qualities of musicianship before focusing exclusively on the nuts and bolts, but to me, it was no different from attending law school after completing a political science major at a liberal arts college. Juilliard narrowed my focus for a time, and once I overcame my allergy to single-mindedness, I enjoyed it. I went on to do a year of postgraduate work at the San Francisco Conservatory of Music. Since graduating, I have stayed in the Bay Area to be close to my family. In my performances, teaching, and producing, I seek always to impart the excitement of discovering connections and the joy of interacting deeply with great works of art.

At another university or conservatory program, I might have had almost any of the individual experiences that I had as a student at Bard, but there is no educational institution, academic or musical, where I could have had Bard's unique combination of experiences. The intersections and conflicts between these experiences taught me how to think critically, how to search for connections and stay open to unexpected ones, and how to communicate my ideas.

But, ultimately, my education at Bard also taught me something more intangible: the importance of exploring my own voice in all its permutations. From my unorthodox audition to the end of my five years in the Conservatory program, I learned to appreciate my own process of learning and working, to hone it, and to trust it. I am no longer afraid to have nebulous dreams, but I also have the tools to shape them into something concrete. I am still discovering my voice and hope it will be a lifelong process. In this unpredictable and ever-changing world, it is a gift to know yourself. Only with that knowledge can we realize our potential and give the best of ourselves and our abilities. Bard showed me how to traverse that path of self-discovery, and I will always be grateful for its guidance.

PART II

CONNECTIONS

Musical "Topics" and Expression in Music

ROBERT MARTIN

I.

In a series of illuminating discussions, Wye Allanbrook has developed the idea that musical commonplaces, or "topics," in Mozart's music shed light on the problem of expression in that music.[1] Topics are, roughly speaking, allusions within a piece of music to well-known kinds of music associated with various social settings, such as the hunt, the courtly dance, religious rituals, etc. Their importance derives from the commonplace nature of these kinds of music. Familiarity with them, and with their associations, could be assumed by Mozart and other composers; so they provided a musical link to the extra-musical.

Allanbrook notes a striking shift from the eighteenth-century view that instrumental music was inferior because without words it lacked the means to "paint the passions," to the nineteenth-century view that purely instrumental music was superior precisely because of its purity. She notes the anomalousness of a prejudice in favor of texted music at a time when such masterworks as Mozart's piano concerti and string quartets were being produced and the unsatisfactory nature of the kind of music analysis that seems required by the nineteenth-century prejudice for "autonomous" music, an analysis that considers only purely musical relations among musical events. Her attractive suggestion is that the topics idea could have helped eighteenth-century theorists understand how, for example, Mozart's string quartets also paint the passions, and can help us, today, feel comfortable with music analysis that takes affect and expression seriously. The topics, which were the shared background knowledge of audiences and composers alike, provide a connection to the feelings and forms of human life associated with the settings to which the topics refer.

My aim in this paper is to understand and evaluate the idea of musical topics as a contribution to the discussion of expression in classic music. Therefore, part of the paper is an analysis of the claims and arguments that lie behind the topics idea, and part is a formulation of my own ideas about expression in music of the classic period. My ideas do not take the form of an answer to what I will call, for lack of a better term, the orthodox problem of expression in music; rather, they take the form of a different approach to the issue, starting with a recommendation that different questions be asked. I will conclude that the topics idea is not helpful if the problem of expression is posed in the orthodox way, but it is helpful if expression is viewed in the way that I recommend.

II.

The orthodox philosophical problem of expression is to explain what it means for a piece of music to express, or be expressive of, some human emotion, such as joy or sorrow. The task is to explain the connection between the *music itself* and the emotions, as opposed to two other phenomena: the expression of a *composer's* emotions through the act of composing and the evocation by music of an emotional response in *listeners*.

Using Mozart's music as an example, let me try to motivate the three-way distinction I am drawing.[2] We can think about Mozart's emotions and the likelihood that one of the things he was doing in composing string quartets was expressing some of his emotions. It is perhaps not unreasonable to think of musical composition as a form of behavior that can serve to express feelings or emotions. From this perspective, we may want to listen to Mozart's music as an indication of what emotions he felt at various times. But it is not clear how we can read information about Mozart's emotions from his music. That the music sounds full of pride is no indication of how he felt when composing it. Perhaps a more promising approach is to try to learn about the kind of pride Mozart experienced, when he did experience it, from the parts of the music that we identify independently as sounding proud. But then it is clear that we are confronting emotions connected somehow to the music itself, recognizable quite independently of hypotheses about Mozart's emotions. That is the connection that the orthodox problem of expression seeks to understand.

We can also think about our own emotions and the quite reasonable notion that a smaller or larger section of a piece of music can induce an emotional response. This is a topic in psychological theory, even if, as in the case of Leonard Meyer, the attempt is made to connect the unfolding of specifically musical events to the arousal of emotions.[3] But the musical work itself is perceived as having an emotional quality, not simply as causing emotional response. So we are led to the question, *what is the connection of the musical work to human emotions?* other than either of the two more straightforward connections concerning the emotions of the composer and the emotions of the listener.[4] This is the key question for the orthodox problem of musical expression.

There are, basically speaking, two groups of answers to this question. Those of the first group hold that musical works have features—melodic contour, tempo, texture, etc.—that resemble the ways that humans experience or express emotions. On the basis of this resemblance, words from the vocabulary of human emotions are thought to be applied metaphorically. Writers in this group include Eduard Hanslick, Monroe Beardsley, and, I suppose, Peter Kivy.[5] Those of the second group hold that there is some kind of semantic relation between music and the emotions or that the very distinction between music and the extra-musical breaks down. Writers in this second group include Susanne Langer, Wye Allanbrook, Lawrence Kramer, Kofi Agawu, and Susan McClary.[6]

III.

Let me turn now to the topics idea, with an eye toward assessing its contribution to solving the orthodox philosophical problem of musical expression. It consists of the following five or six claims:

1. A collection of easily recognizable kinds of music was widely known to Mozart and his audiences. Some examples are:

> music of the hunt
> courtly music marches
> courtly music fanfares
> social dance music (e.g., Laendler, minuet, bourrée, contredanse)
> music box and mechanical clock music
> church music (learned style)
> "concertante"(virtuoso) music
> "sensitive style" music
> hurdy-gurdy music
> "Turkish" music

I have restricted myself to examples of what I would call the narrow range: each is associated with a particular kind of social occasion or setting. This fits one of Allanbrook's characterizations: "In music the term has been borrowed [from the field of rhetoric] to designate 'commonplace' musical styles or figures whose expressive connotations, derived from the circumstances in which they are habitually employed, are familiar to all."[7] It also fits one of her later characterizations: "a ready-to-hand vocabulary of musical expression gathered from the simpler music written to accompany daily activities: court life, worship, the hunt."[8] Some of the examples I have excluded are:

> "types of basses like the descending-tetrachord or chaconne, associated with lament and the antique";
> "the minor mode, which is a special affect for Classic composers, not a mode of expression parallel to the major";
> "the wind serenade sound, so prevalent in Mozart's piano sonatas";
> "the tune . . . an effective stabilizing force."[9]

I would suggest that such excluded examples are something quite different. The minor mode and the wind serenade sound are not intuitively on a par with music of the church, of the dance, of the hunt; they are not kinds of music that are associated with particular settings. I think such examples are included, mistakenly, in the "topics" account because they do have something important in common with topics proper—they are independently recognizable musical materials, some of which have a recognizable function. This is why there is less definiteness about how to individuate examples of this kind and the absence of what Allanbrook calls "fortunate names."[10] Later, when I have argued that topics are special cases of a more general category, it will seem natural, I hope, to hold the topics account to examples in which a kind of music is associated with a familiar social activity.

2. These kinds of music have associations, derived from the situations in which they are habitually employed.

Allanbrook calls these "expressive connotations," but for our purposes, that begs two questions: (1) whether expression is really involved; and (2) whether one should look upon bits of music, such as a fanfare or hunt call, as capable of having connotations (and denotations). I will incorporate the notion of expression later in my reconstruction of the topics idea. As for connotation, the examples suggest that the term is used loosely to indicate something secondary: the kind of music in question is the horn call of the hunt and therefore "connotes" (is associated with) such things as the outdoors, the excitement of the chase, etc.

It is difficult to say just what these associations are, and I have not in fact seen them made explicit. I would venture the following examples:

> music of the hunt: associated with the outdoors, good cheer and excitement of the chase, good health, upper-class amusement;
> courtly marches and fanfares: associated with military esprit, patriotic fervor, parades, pageantry;
> minuet music: associated with elegance, perhaps restrained sexuality;
> church and learned music: associated with religious feelings, sophistication;
> "concertante (virtuoso music): associated with charismatic attractiveness;
> "sensitive style" music: associated with intimacy, the drawing room;
> hurdy-gurdy music: associated with the lower classes, street entertainment;
> "Turkish" music: associated with the exotic Orient.

3. The associations were common knowledge in Mozart's time, and Mozart was aware of the fact that they were common knowledge.

4. Mozart's music contains passages that are very abbreviated examples of these kinds, and that would have been recognized as such by his audiences.

This is a special case of the more general and very interesting phenomenon: musical quotations. In our case, what is quoted are bits of music of a certain recognizable kind that is associated with extra-musical activities; in other cases what is quoted are bits of music written by other composers or from folk traditions or from earlier works of the same composer.[11]

5. These passages constitute allusions, or references, to the kinds of music in question; to them are transferred the associations held by the musical topics.

For example, a half-measure of fifths and thirds is an allusion to the music of the hunt and has associations with the outdoors, etc.

So far it seems to me that each of these claims is plausible and, as I have said, illuminating taken together. What we have is a clear conception of a range of musical materials available to Mozart and used by him, providing association-laden connections to the extra-musical world. But there is the further claim, relevant to the question of expression:

6. By means of such allusions a Mozart work can be said to "paint the passions," i.e., to express emotions.

The argument for 6 seems to be that the passions—not idiosyncratic personal feelings but rather universal and generic feelings—are present in the music through the connection of these feelings to the settings or the associations of the musical topics. "From their connections to the noble, middle-class, and humble, the pious and impious, whatever is proud or abased, tranquil or restless, antique or modern, in these occasions they draw their referential power and their affect."[12] This claim goes beyond the idea of the topics as a distinctive part of Mozart's compositional resources; it is a claim about the orthodox philosophical problem of expression.

Viewed as such, I think that the claim is unsuccessful. To begin with, the examples offer nothing beyond what we have already in claims 1 to 5: that the use of topics brings with it associations from certain social settings. Even if, in some cases, these associations have to do with human emotions, it does not follow that the music expresses or refers to these emotions. Suppose, for example, that feelings of health and good cheer are associated with the music of the hunt. One can imagine Mozart very effectively imbedding an allusion to the hunt in a passage of nostalgic sadness; in such a passage the use of the topic surely does not amount to expression of health and good cheer. On the negative side, it would seem that most of the topics, whatever their function, are neutral with respect to emotion: for example, learned style music, "sensitive style" music, "Turkish" music. Some pieces of music that are clearly expressive of sadness and grief, if any are, such as the introduction to the last movement of Mozart's G-Minor String Quintet (K. 516), do not, as far as I can tell, contain any topics of the narrow range; even if they do, it is implausible to suppose that the topics are responsible for the expression of sadness. Topics are neither sufficient nor necessary for the expression of emotions, and their possible association with the emotional coloring of certain social settings does not imply anything like the "painting of the passions."[13]

I suggest that the real and important effect of the topics is to give to the work a feeling of being connected to other experiences of life: the court, the hunt, church-going, etc. This accounts for something very important in the experience of many listeners—the feeling that even "abstract" music has close connections to the fullness of life's experiences. It is, exactly as Allanbrook says in the conference paper, an understanding of music's "connection to the world" (p. 7) that is the value of the topics idea, and this is quite independent, I think, of any claim about the expression of emotions.

IV.

I characterized the orthodox philosophical problem of musical expression as flowing from the question, *what is the connection between a musical work and human emotions?* Perhaps that is the wrong question to begin with. J. L. Austin, in 'A Plea for Excuses,"[14] suggested that we ask not about grand and intractable concepts, such as moral responsibility, but about such humbler topics as excuses. I want to approach the notion of expressiveness in music by asking not about the connection to human emotions, but with a humbler question: What is meant by expressive playing? All would admit the importance of performance in our experience of music and the fact that some players are particularly expressive players; I think we can get at, at least roughly, what that means. The question is whether we can find our way from that to the broader question about expressiveness in music where more of importance to the experience of listeners is at stake.

We ask, then, what is meant by expressive playing? An expressive player stresses certain notes, lingers at certain points in a phrase, moves ahead at other points, varies tone color and dynamics in response to varying chords or harmonies, sustains phrases to their conclusions, paces crescendi and diminuendi to maintain tension, marks the color change from major to minor, brings out the contrast between allusions to the church and to the virtuoso soloist, and so on.

I recall that as music students we used to mock the following idea about learning a new, difficult work: first we should learn the notes, then the rhythms, then add the dynamics, and finally add the expression. As silly as this was, it was perfectly plain to us all what it meant: that there could be the correct series of pitches; there could be a rhythmically precise performance, all at mezzo-forte; perhaps most clearly of all, because all too often actually encountered, there could be a note-perfect but inexpressive performance. We realized that even if accents, hair-pins, and other expression marks were observed literally, the performance could be lacking in "real" expression; real expression required a certain sensitive, responsive realization even of the expression marks themselves. The point to be noticed in all of this, I believe, is that the performer's expressiveness is in some peculiar way separable from the composer's instructions.[15] No separation will be apparent in an actual, convincing performance, but the conceptual distinction is important.

If we think again of the characterization of an expressive performer, we notice that the unifying thread is responsiveness to the raw materials: tonality, rhythm, the structure of melodies, and, I would add, the topics, since these too are among the materials at a composer's disposal. This connection with the materials of music would explain the feeling that expressive playing operates at a level that is somehow distinct from that of the works themselves. It is striking in this connection that expressive performers can play expressively even when sight-reading. This is noted by E. F. Clarke and commented on as follows: "These observations mean that expression . . . must be regarded as being generated from the performer's understanding of the musical structure."[16] If by "musical structure" Clarke means the structure of the musical work, then his conclusion is implausible; it seems more reasonable to explain expressive sight-reading as derived from the performer's ability to respond to that which is in some sense prior to the musical work, for example, the expressive properties of intervals and chords or the expressive properties of aspects of the style in which the work is written.

To give substance to this idea that expressiveness has to do with a response to the materials of music, I need to say more about these materials. What is it about the materials of music that leads us to say that when a performer responds to them the performance is expressive? Let me give a single, very simple example. There is something important about the interval of the octave, and this importance is to a large extent natural (as opposed to constructed). What makes the octave an important natural phenomenon is that the most prominent overtones of any given tone are those at exactly twice the frequency of the starting tone (that is, at the octave). Therefore, relative to any tone, the octave is the tone that is most consonant—most supported, or reinforced, by the overtones of the starting tone. I do not doubt that the octave plays widely varying roles in various musics of the world and that some of the particular importance or significance that the octave has in Western music is "constructed"; but it does seem evident that it has a physical basis of great importance. One has only to sing a pitch and then let one's voice go up, seeking a stable point of rest, to feel the force of this point.

How the octave is divided is far less natural—the division of the octave into twelve roughly equal semitones that characterizes the Western modes is not at all universal. Each of the modes is a particular arrangement of semitones and whole tones, and tonality, as it stabilized in the seventeenth century, is the selection of two of these arrangements, known now as major and minor. Tonality, then, is certainly a construct, and therefore a worthy subject, of cultural theory—one wonders, and many have speculated on, what other cultural phenomena of the seventeenth century are related to the construction of tonality. But tonality is a construct with a physical basis; there are relevant acoustical facts, at least partially determinative of the importance of the octave.

To come now to the example, consider the difference between the third degree of the major scale and the lowered third degree—the changed tone that distinguishes the minor from the major triad. The characteristic of the example should be instantly clear: the lowered third has a particular "dynamic quality," to use Zuckerkandl's term,[17] that we can express metaphorically by saying that it wants to go down, that it pulls down, to the second degree of the scale; while the major third has somewhat more equilibrium—if anything, it seems to want to go up to the fourth degree of the scale. Our characterization of the dynamic quality of these tones is of necessity metaphorical and anthropomorphic, because the quality itself is primitive in the sense of not being definable in simpler terms.

We have here a fascinating and perplexing feature of our environment: when perceived within a tonal context, a tone is felt to have a particular, very distinctive property. However, one has only to alter the context, and the property is altered. Because tonality is involved, and not only acoustic facts, the phenomenon must be regarded as partly constructed, partly "natural." It is indeed the phenomenon of "hearing as," treated by Wittgenstein in the *Philosophical Investigations*; in the key of C one hears the E-flat as pulling down a half-step; one hears the E natural as lifting toward F. Similarly, one sees three horizontal lines encircled as a human face.[18] It is arguable that one cannot *not* see the lines as a face, that this is a fact of human psychology; nor, for some reason, can one, in C major, not hear the E-flat as pulling down. The basis here will be at least partly acoustic rather than psychological; presumably, the perceived disequilibrium of the E-flat is at least partly the result of the fact that the major third matches one of the fairly strong overtones of the tonic, while the minor third matches no such overtone.

This, then, is my example of a bit of the material of music to which an expressive player may be expected to respond. But why "expressive"? It is one thing for there to be some acoustic fact or some "dynamic quality" of pitches or rhythms to which a sensitive player responds; so far, one might call the performer's response simply "revelatory." More is required for the performer's response to the stuff of music to be called expressive; this presumably requires that the musical qualities to which the performer responds be expressively colored in some sense to be made clear.

In the case of our example, one can speculate on why the minor is perceived as expressively colored, perhaps darker or sadder than the major. The downward pull of the minor third, that contour, is similar to features of human expressive behavior associated with downcast moods: most obviously and literally, the intonation contour of the voice of a person experiencing the emotion of sadness.[19] (Though there is, I believe, this similarity between the dynamic quality of the tones and features of human expressive behavior, it does not follow that the lowered third is always perceived as having this expressive coloration—the association is certainly defeasible.)

The range of expressively charged materials is enormous, from such relatively simple examples as the timbral complexity of the open C string of the cello at the "natural" end of the spectrum, to aspects of compositional styles and conventions that become part of the language of well-versed players and listeners at the constructed end of the spectrum. An example of the latter is this: a performer may, even in sight-reading, play the opening melody of a work that appears to be theme and variations with a kind of simplicity and neutrality, knowing, as part of his or her knowledge of the style, that the theme will unfold and blossom and intensify as the work proceeds. The neutral statement of the theme will allow this unfolding to be more clearly perceived by listeners.

I am suggesting, as others have before me, that there is a level of pre-compositional material charged with expressive potential to which members of the musical community are sensitive. Composers shape this material, taking advantage of its expressive potential and counting on the sensitivities of performers and listeners. It is not the work, then, that is, in the first instance, expressive, but rather the stuff of music. That is perhaps why one feels discomfort in saying—or, for that matter, in denying—that a substantial section of a work is, for example, sad or joyous. The reality is fine-grained, moment-to-moment expressiveness. Perhaps, to put it differently, one hears in a work what is done to—what happens to—expressive materials; one listens to where the composer takes those materials.[20] Within our musical environment and, a fortiori, as part of the composer's vocabulary, the materials already have expressive meaning; the interest is not so much in what is expressed but rather in what develops.

It needs to be emphasized, against the impression I may have given so far, that in the best case the performer's response is not simply to the materials of music but to these materials as employed by the composer. Expressiveness is certainly not only the work of the performer. The composer uses the expressive potential of the musical materials, and the performer responds to those materials in the context of the work.

For example, a performer will pay less heed to particular expressive opportunities in an extended, building section of a piece, for fear that the sense of continuation and heightening will be disrupted; the very same expressive opportunities occurring elsewhere in the piece will be brought out more fully. A second example, this one real: in the Minuet movement of Mozart's K. 421 Quartet, the opening trumpet-call dotted rhythm of the cello and violin 1 in octaves has a troubled, even anguished character (playing against the usual rhetoric of the figure), caused by the fact that the movement is in D minor (after an F-major slow movement) and by the relatively high register of the cello part (a two-octave spread between violin 1 and cello would sound very different indeed) and by the continuation of the line in the inner voices. The performer seeks a kind of collaborative relationship with the composer in grasping and projecting to the audience the intentions of the composer, including the composer's use of preexisting materials.

Again, neither the performer nor the composer is the primary source of expressiveness: it is the musical material—its extra-musical significance—that is primary. The composer takes advantage of the potential of the material, and the performer responds to the potential in real time and to real effect.

I characterized the orthodox philosophical problem of musical expression as the question: What does it mean to say that a musical work expresses, or is expressive of, happiness or sadness? My response was to turn away from that question and to ask other questions, for example, about expressive playing. But where are we left with respect to the orthodox problem? On the one hand, it seems that almost nothing is conveyed by saying that a musical work, or even a short section of a musical work, expresses, or is expressive of, happiness or sadness. Such a statement seems too crude to do justice to our musical experience. Our account of the expressive playing of expressive works seems not to require that some emotion be expressed by the work. On the other hand, I am not about to deny that a scherzo can be joyous.

Perhaps a fruitful direction in which to explicate such statements is suggested by the ideas put forward here: perhaps such characterizations can usefully be traced back to the expressive potential of the musical materials, including topics, available for the use of a composer, as these materials are understood and felt by all members of the musical community.

To summarize: I have suggested that the topics idea is an extremely valuable tool for our understanding of classic music, because it explains our feelings about the connections of the music to the association-laden situations of daily life. I have argued further that the topics are a special case of the category of musical materials that exist independently of particular works; some of these materials, but not all of the topics, have strong emotional coloring and may lie at the root of the phenomenon of expressiveness in music. It is in this sense that I can see a connection between topics and expression.

NOTES

1. See her *Rhythmic Gesture in Mozart: Le Nozze di Figaro and Don Giovanni* (University of Chicago Press, 1983) and "'Ear-Tickling Nonsense': A New Context for Musical Expression in Mozart's 'Haydn' Quartets," *The St. John's Review* 38 (1988): 1–24. I base my remarks also on her paper "Expression in Mozart's String Quartets" presented at a UCLA conference in April 1992 (unpublished manuscript). Allanbrook credits Leonard G. Ratner, *Classic Music: Expression, Form, and Style* (New York: Schirmer Books, 1980) with the first extended modern discussion of topics in music. A recent analytical work that makes much of the notion of topics is Kofi Agawu, *Playing with Signs: A Semiotic Analysis of Classic Music* (Princeton University Press, 1991).

2. This is set out clearly in Peter Kivy, *The Corded Shell: Reflections on Musical Expression* (Princeton University Press, 1980), pp. 3–4.

3. Leonard Meyer, *Emotion and Meaning in Music* (University of Chicago Press, 1956).

4. In the case of the visual arts, Richard Wollheim has argued persuasively (in *Painting as an Art* [Princeton University Press, 1987]) for a view that strongly connects the emotions of the painter and the viewer to the emotional content of the painting. Roughly

speaking, the painter, positioned to gauge the work's effect on a spectator, creates meaning in the work by producing marks intended to have a certain effect and intended to be perceived as flowing from such an intention. I believe this picture can be applied illuminatingly to music. But even with this account of the interconnected nature of creator's and audience's emotion, there appears to remain the need for an account of the work's own expressiveness; indeed, Wollheim offers such an account for painting in terms of the psychological phenomenon of projection.

5. Eduard Hanslick, *On the Musically Beautiful: A Contribution towards the Revision of the Aesthetics of Music*, trans. Geoffrey Payzant (1891; reprint, Indianapolis: Hackett Publishing Co., 1986). Monroe Beardsley, "Understanding Music" in Kingsley Price, ed., *On Criticizing Music* (Johns Hopkins University Press, 1981). Kivy, *The Corded Shell*. Kivy holds, more exactly, that the assertion that a theme is "broken with grief" should be construed as saying that the theme is expressive of grief (as opposed to: expresses grief; the latter but not the former is thought to require that the grief be experienced). The features of the music that support this characterization are just those that belong to what Monroe Beardsley calls "human regional qualities." It can perhaps be argued that the attribution of "expressive of grief" to a piece of music is a metaphorical extension of the literal attribution of that phrase (to something that could also be expressing grief).

6. Susanne K. Langer, *Philosophy in a New Key* (Harvard University Press, 1942). Lawrence Kramer, *Music as Cultural Practice, 1800–1900* (University of California Press, 1993). Agawu, *Playing with Signs*. Susan McClary, "Narrative Agendas in 'Absolute' Music: Identity and Difference in Brahms's Third Symphony," in Ruth Solie, ed., *Musicology and Difference* (University of California Press, 1993).

7. *Rhythmic Gesture in Mozart*, p. 329, n. 4.

8. "'Ear-Tickling Nonsense,'" p. 12.

9. Agawu, in *Playing with Signs*, p. 30, includes in his list of topics such things as *alla breve*.

10. "Expression," p. 12. Similarly, with examples from this broader range there is the temptation to fill in stretches of music that seem to be topic-free with artifacts of the theory (see Agawu, *Playing with Signs*, p. 49).

11. See Charles Rosen, "Influence: Plagiarism and Inspiration" in K. Price, ed., *On Criticizing Music*, pp. 16-37. In this kind of allusion, to the delight of the connoisseur, the actual bit of music quoted is less likely to have general significance (because it is not associated with a social situation); Rosen suggests that the significance in some cases resides not in the passage alluded to, but in the fact of allusion ("The two opening references to Beethoven's "Emperor" Concerto [in Brahms's Piano Concerto No. 2] . . . must be understood as staking a claim. This work, we are informed by these opening references, is intended to follow upon the tradition left off by Beethoven" [p. 27]). The other major difference is that the allusion is unlikely to be understood by very many—even if Rosen is right that "Brahms was a master of allusion, and . . . generally intended his references to be heard" (p. 26).

12. "'Ear-Tickling Nonsense,'" p. 12. In "Expression" Allanbrook offers a more inclusive account of music's painting of the passions: "In music passions can be projected by appropriate rhythms and figures. . . . Through its harmony and rhythm, bound with historical associations with the lament and the ecclesiastical styles, it stirs in its auditors cognition of the affect of the noble pathetic, one of the many motions of the human soul" (p. 15). In this more inclusive account, the topics' part of the explanation ("historical associations with the lament and the ecclesiastical styles") is mingled with the traditional appeal to natural similarities between elements of harmony and rhythm and types of human emotions. I am concerned here only with the explanatory contribution of the topics.

13. A referee of this journal has raised another problem with the topics account as a response to the orthodox problem of expression: that it fails to explain how a competent listener today recognizes the expressive properties of (say) Mozart's music. Surely many topics have long since ceased to be commonplace. But I do not take the topic theorist to claim that topics are the only basis for expression in music; I suppose that a topic theorist would simply agree that a good deal of background knowledge is necessary to appreciate topics and that this in part accounts for the fact that educated listeners "get more" from hearing performances.

14. Proceedings of the Aristotelian Society 57 (1956–57): 1-30.

15. *The Concise Oxford Dictionary of Music*, 3rd ed. (London: Oxford University Press, 1980) defines "expression" as "that part of a composer's music such as subtle nuances of dynamics which he has no full means of committing to paper and must leave to the artistic perception and insight of the executant."

16. "Expression and Communication in Musical Performance," in Johan Sundberg, Lennart Nord, and Rolf Carlson, eds., *Music, Language, Speech and Brain* (London: Macmillan, 1991), pp. 184–193.

17. Victor Zuckerkandl, *Sound and Symbol: Music and the External World* (Princeton University Press, 1956), pp. 11 ff.

18. See, for example, *Philosophical Investigations* (New York: The Macmillan Company, 1953), I, 534. Wittgenstein compares understanding a sentence with understanding a theme in music at I, 527. The phenomenon of "seeing-as" is treated more extensively in the *Investigations*, for example at II, xi.

19. See Kivy, *The Corded Shell*, chaps. 1–5.

20. I owe this thought to Robert Marshall.

Soufflé in A Minor

ANDRÉ ACIMAN

In her classic *Mastering the Art of French Cooking*, Julia Child explains how to fold a mixture when preparing a soufflé. "First," she writes, "stir a big spoonful of egg whites into the soufflé mixture to lighten it. Then with a rubber scraper, scoop the rest of the egg whites on top. Finally, still using your rubber scraper, cut down from the top center of the mixture to the bottom of the saucepan, then draw the scraper quickly toward you against the edge of the pan, and up to the left and out. You are thus bringing a bit of the mixture at the bottom of the pan up over the egg whites. Continue the movement while slowly rotating the saucepan, and cutting down, toward you, and out to the left, until the egg whites have been folded into the body of the soufflé. The whole process should not take more than a minute, and do not attempt to be too thorough. It is better to leave few unblended patches than to deflate the egg whites."

The whipped egg whites, in case the chef was not clear, are nothing more than trapped air.

What Julia Child has in mind is a sort of zigzagging, figure-eight movement of the rubber scraper, which takes the mixture to the top, folds it back toward the bottom, then takes what was just folded to the top again. Call this layering, not moving forward or backward, just stationary wrist motions, the equivalent, say, of treading water without budging in a swimming pool. What was at the top is folded to the bottom, then folded sideways and back up again.

And this, to stretch a point, is pure Beethoven. Toward the end of a quartet, a sonata, a symphony, Beethoven takes a string of notes, whatever string it is, repeats it, folds it in, again and again, not going anywhere with it, yet always careful never to deflate it, and, summoning up all his creative genius, he plays for time until the end—except that when he reaches the end, he will find some way to uncover newer musical opportunities, if only to keep on folding and refolding again. *You thought I was done and expected a resounding, clamorous close,* he says, *but I halted the process, kept you suspended for a very short while, and then came back with more, sometimes much more, and made you wish I'd never stop.* The close of many pieces has these moments of mounting repetition, a sudden arrest that looks like the announcement of a last breath and a closing cadenza, only then to hear Beethoven utter a new promise, folding again and again, until the listener longs for perpetuity—as though the purpose of all music were not to seek closure but to come up with new ways to put off closure.

At the level of plot, literature tries to do this all the time. A detective novel or a serialized novel is dilatory at its very core. It creates opportunities for hasty resolutions only then to surprise the reader with deceptive clues, mistaken assumptions, unexpected deferrals, and cliff-hangers. Suspense and surprise are as essential to both prose and music as are revelation and resolution. Bram Stoker's *Dracula* is punctuated by endless setbacks and unforeseen delays. Jane Austen's *Emma,* on the other hand, could so easily have ended midway when it became clear to the reader that Emma Woodhouse had a crush on Frank Churchill, and that he too was seemingly stricken. This would have been an acceptable ending, and the first time I remember reading the novel I was entirely persuaded that this is where the novel was indeed headed. I was wrong, and Austen, rather than end with the marriage of these two would-be lovers, decided to reject this plausible ending and go in search of another and, having proposed this other ending, discarded it for yet another.

Music is far more adept at this because it can fold and refold numberless times. Literature cannot. Barring plot, however, there are similar stylistic instances in literature, and I would like to mention two: Joyce and Proust.

Among the most beautiful and most musical passages in the English language are the closing pages of James Joyce's "The Dead." They are the most musical, not only because of their cadence—when read aloud, they'll persuade anyone of the stunningly lyrical, anaphoric beauty of Joyce's prose—but also because the story itself does not end when it should. The story, in fact, has already ended before it ends, except that Joyce wasn't quite done yet and, like Beethoven, simply kept going, withholding the full stop, folding one clause into the next, again and again, as if in search of a closure that he wasn't finding but wasn't going to give up on, because the search for closure and cadence was not incidental to what he was writing but its true drama, its true plot. Rhythm, in this instance, is not subsidiary to the story of Greta and Gabriel or to the portrait of the elderly aunts on the Feast of the Epiphany; it becomes the story. If every reader recalls "The Dead," it is precisely because the rhythm of its closing pages totally transcends what would have simply been the longest and chattiest tale of *Dubliners*.

I've always suspected that Joyce had no idea how to close "The Dead"—a seemingly rudderless tale—and stumbled on its final segment simply because he had waited for something to happen and had the genius to make room for it, to leave open spaces for it, even when he didn't know what might come to fill that space or where the story might take him once he had indeed filled those spaces. All he knew perhaps was that closure would most likely have something to do with snow. He had the genius not to give up waiting. Waiting for something to happen, avoiding hasty closure, deferring the period, opening up space for the unknown visitor, trying out seemingly pointless clauses provided they adhered to a particular rhythm—this was genius. Call it, if not folding, then padding, or to use Walter Pater's word for it, surplussage, or, in keeping the soufflé analogy, trapping air. Real meaning, real art, does not necessarily reside in the nitty-gritty, bare rag and bone shop of the heart; it resides just as easily in the seemingly superfluous, in the extra, in the joy of folding and refolding air. Making room for the unexpected visitor, the extra who, in this case, happened to be a young man called Michael Furey who shows up almost adventitiously at the tail end of the story.

Taking one's time, folding and refolding with no clear sense of where exactly one might be headed, trapping air bubbles, making extra room for things that have yet to come brings up another metaphor: the nineteenth-century Russian chemist Dmitri Mendeleyev, who invented the periodic table of elements and was able to arrange the elements of our planet by their weight, valence, and behavior. Mendeleyev created several columns in his table and proved that elements layered under the same column might have different atomic weights but would still share the same valence and hence react to other elements in similar ways. Thus Lithium, Sodium, and Potassium, with atomic numbers 3, 11, and 19, might have different atomic weights, but all share a valence of $+1$, while Oxygen, Sulfur, and Selenium, with atomic numbers 8, 16, and 34, have a valence of -2. Mendeleyev was so sure of his discovery—and this is the purpose of the analogy here—that he left empty "boxes" on his table for those elements that had yet to be found.

Mendeleyev's table not only attributed an ineluctable, rational sequence to what might otherwise have seemed a random arrangement of elements on Planet Earth but also offered something more than an ineluctable, rational sequence: an aesthetic design. Design itself transcends the sequence, transcends the elements of chemistry, transcends melody and counterpoint, transcends the story of Joyce's dinner on the Feast of the Epiphany. Design and rhythm themselves becomes the subject of the sequence. In the creation of empty, tentative boxes on the periodic table, or in the endless, exploratory folding and unfolding of musical phrases or verbal clauses, the chemist-composer-writer is in fact operating under the spell of three things: design, discovery, and deferral.

By folding and refolding, layer after layer, art hopes to restore order on the fringes of chaos. And if *restore* is the wrong verb, then let's say that by folding and refolding, art tries to *impose* or, at best, to *invent* order. Art is an interpretation of chaos. Art is the discovery and the revelation of meaning through form. By folding and refolding, artists create the opportunity for invoking a deeper layer of order and harmony, one that goes further yet than the original design that the artist was so pleased to have created. The joy of discovering design by dint of waiting for it not just at the level of plot, but also at the level of style, is perhaps the pinnacle of artistic achievement. Art is always about discovery and design and a reasoning with chaos.

And here perhaps we should turn to Marcel Proust, who, exactly like Joyce, was not only devoted to music but also a master stylist. Proust's sentence is recognizable because it operates on three levels: the start is frequently a muted afflatus, a moment of inspiration or uplift, an insight or idea that needs to be elaborated and examined and that sets the course of the sentence. The end of the sentence, however, is entirely different. A Proustian sentence normally closes with a fillip, what in French is called a *pointe*, or, in Latin, a *clausula*: a burst of revelation, a short, almost caustic dart that uncovers something altogether surprising and unforeseen and unsaddles every expectation the reader might have had.

The middle of the sentence is where folding occurs. Here Proust allows the sentence to tarry and swell with intercalated material that proceeds ever so cautiously, sometimes forced to fork, and to fork again while opening up subsidiary parenthetical clauses along the way, until, after much deliberation, unannounced, having acquired enough air and ballast along the way, the sentence suddenly unleashes the closing fillip. Proust's sentence needs this middle zone. Like a huge wave, the sentence needs to swell and build momentum—sometimes with totally negligible material—before finally crashing against the shore. Proust's *clausula* reverses and capsizes all that preceded. It is the ultimate product of continued folding and refolding, of the persistent trapping of air. It is how Proust seeks out the possibility of a miracle. It's also how he holds out for what he does not yet know, cannot yet see, and has no sense he'll even end up writing.

All artists labor to see *other* than what's given to be seen; they want to see more, to let form summon up things that were hitherto unseen and that only form, not knowledge or experience, could have foreseen. Art is not just the product of labor, it is the love of laboring with unknown possibilities. Art is not our attempt to capture experience and give it a form but to let form itself discover experience, to let form become experience. Art may very well be the attempt to dispose of an obsession, but art already knows that the obsession will not go away, that it will come back, partly because an obsession can't really work itself out on paper, on a score sheet, on a canvass, or in the kitchen—it always comes back—but also because art is the pleasurable process that takes over the obsession and becomes obsessive on its own and therefore never really wants the original obsession dispelled. Art resuscitates the obsession in order to make it go away again and again and again.

And in this I am reminded of what is probably Beethoven's most beautiful piece of music: the *Heiliger Dankgesang eines Genesenen an die Gottheit, in der lydischen Tonart*, composed after a close bout with sickness and death. The *Song of Thanksgiving* is a handful of notes, plus a sustained, overextended hymn in the Lydian mode, which the composer loves and doesn't wish to see end, because he likes repeating questions and deferring answers, because all answers are easy, because it's not answers or clarity, or even ambiguity, that Beethoven wants. What he is after is deferral and distended time, a grace period that never expires and that comes like memory, but is not memory, all cadence with nary hint of the scariest chaos awaiting next door, called death. And Beethoven will keep repeating and extending the process until he is left with five notes, three notes, one note, no note, no breath. And maybe all art is just that, life without death.

Music and Social Responsibility: Remembering the Genocide of European Roma during World War II

ÁDÁM FISCHER

In October 2014, Hungarian conductor Ádám Fischer conducted a performance of the Mozart Requiem at Bard College in memory of European Roma killed 70 years earlier at Auschwitz. The event included a panel discussion, "History and Responsibility," with speakers Ádám Fischer, Constantin Iordachi, Margareta Matache, and Erika Schlager. Mr. Fischer wrote the following essay as an introduction to this memorial event.

The Porajmos—the World War II genocide of Sinti and Roma—reached its bloody climax 70 years ago in a night in which innocents were tortured and murdered because of their race. Women and men, children and old people were brutally killed with machine guns and flamethrowers.

By 1944 the Nazi concentration camp at Auschwitz was overflowing, with no place to put incoming prisoners. On August 2 of that year, in order to make space, the Nazi authorities moved to eliminate the so-called Gypsy Camp in Auschwitz.

It is our duty, our responsibility, to remember these events, and I am grateful to Bard College for assisting me in organizing a special program that honors and remembers these victims.

Little is known about the martyrdom of the Roma and Sinti during World War II. This chapter of Nazi barbarism seems neglected, even among scholars. Indeed, there is a trend to downplay the victimhood, with even the terminology contested: some scholars argue that the term Holocaust should not encompass the Porajmos at all, but rather be restricted to the Nazi genocide of the Jews.

The Roma genocide has not received the attention it deserves for several reasons, including anti-Romani racism that exists to this day. There is, however, an even more sinister reason lurking beneath the surface, one that goes a long way in explaining the lack of scrutiny and investigation, and one that is particularly relevant today.

Deportation and killing of Gypsy populations in German-occupied territories was often undertaken not under the orders of German occupiers but at the initiative of the local authorities. Across Europe, from France in the west to my native Hungary and the Balkans further east, local administrators seized the moment to rid themselves of their unwanted Gypsy populations. The Nazis occupied Hungary in March 1944. By this stage of the war, the Germans were interested only in deporting Jews. Not one written document points to the Nazis' demanding action against Hungary's Roma; nonetheless, Hungary started arresting and deporting them.

This could be a reason why European (especially Eastern European) societies today feel so uncomfortable remembering the Porajmos. If you cannot blame the Germans alone, better not to speak of it, lest you move from victim to perpetrator. The genocide of the Sinti and Roma peoples was not solely a Nazi crime, it was a European crime. This makes it hard to remember. This is why we must remember.

These days, the very racism that fed into these crimes against humanity is on the rise again, as if we have learned nothing from the past. Across Europe, from France, to Hungary, to Greece, ethnic minorities are made scapegoats for social and economic ills, and politicians ruthlessly exploit this resentment and stoke the flames of racial hatred. In France, the Front National is openly hostile to Sinti and Roma, demanding deportations and incarcerations. In Hungary the situation is even worse, with racists overtly calling for "the elimination of all Gypsies." And politicians see that anti-Roma slogans earn votes in France, Hungary, or Greece, while defending the Roma does not.

A civil society must offer a countering narrative, must remind us of uncomfortable truths, and act as our collective conscience. Our event at Bard College is about remembering the Porajmos, and also about reminding students—young musicians—that as artists we have a unique role to play in society, a special social responsibility. We are privileged because people pay attention to us; they listen to what we have to say. I believe that our duty as artists is to use our position to help those at the margins of our society to be heard: offer our voices in support, fight suppression and repression, further understanding, and give hope. I want to impart that sense of purpose, that calling, to the next generation.

I am happy that we are having this event here in the United States. U.S. society has also battled with the demons of racism and segregation, and great progress has been made in the past 50 years. Despite all its recent turbulence, the United States is still seen as a symbol of hope by many, especially in Eastern Europe. Indeed, the peoples of Eastern Europe follow what happens here very closely. In contrast, sadly, the plight of the Sinti and Roma is not very well known here. My wish is that we help, by shining a light on this dark chapter of human history, by sparking dialogue and countering indifference here in the United States, and by sending a message to Romani around the world that they are not alone. What we do here—our voices and our music—are part of that message.

Music and the New Face of Culture in Nineteenth-Century Europe*

JERROLD SEIGEL

Because the Bard College Conservatory of Music is well known for its dedication to assuring that young performers at the highest level educate themselves in some second field of knowledge, its tenth anniversary provides a fitting moment to ponder music's relationship to neighboring domains of culture, considering both what it may share with them and what sets it apart.

Nineteenth-century Europe provides an especially appropriate focus for such reflection, because it was both a great age of musical composition and performance, and a significant moment in the history of culture more generally. The age of Beethoven, Brahms, Wagner, Verdi, Debussy, and their contemporaries was also the time when the modern sense of the term *culture* became firmly established. In earlier times, culture was most often looked upon as a process, a synonym for mental cultivation that still echoed with its original sense as tilling the soil. During the nineteenth century, the word shifted toward the more concrete sense common today, as the domain of literature and the arts, including the range of activities and objects that belong to it. (The other modern meaning of culture, as the "whole way of life" of some human group, now became more prominent too, but we must leave that aside here.)

Several developments contributed to this shift in meaning. One was the emphasis Europeans placed on the differences between "civilized" societies such as their own and what they regarded as the less developed ones existing elsewhere (a distinction that often served to justify the West's colonial domination of other parts of the globe). A second was

*This essay draws on material treated at greater length in my book *Modernity and Bourgeois Life* (Cambridge, England, and New York, 2012), Chapter 12, where citations are given to the primary and secondary sources on which this essay relies.

the contrast stressed by English writers such as Matthew Arnold between "culture" as a realm devoted to the highest human values, and "civilization," a sphere whose "progress" posed a threat to those values, by dint of its reliance on merely material improvement and the practical techniques that fostered it.

But there was also a third reason behind the emergence of culture in the modern sense, namely the great expansion of intellectual and artistic activities—newspaper and book publishing, museums and exhibitions, concerts and performances—that took place from around 1800, and the changed visage all these phenomena presented as a result. On the one hand, the arts as a whole came to have a larger and more palpable presence in public life and social experience; but this same expansion was part of what gave them a new kind of impact on people's inner, personal lives. As music participated in this transformation, it took on common features with literature and the visual arts, but it also acquired the power to affect people in ways special to itself.

All these developments had their roots in the eighteenth century, but they became more prominent and palpable in the nineteenth. The number of books and pamphlets published in both France and Germany grew by factors of five to ten after around 1715, and historians speak about a "surge" or "explosion" of reading in England by the end of the eighteenth century. The process was greatly amplified from around 1830 by the appearance of cheap newspapers, their reduced prices supported by advertising, and drawing a readership as much as twenty times greater than their predecessors. Some of these sheets, beginning with Émile de Girardin's Parisian *La Presse* in 1836, published serial novels as *feuilletons* at the bottom of the front page, making such writers as Victor Hugo, Eugène Sue, and Honoré de Balzac part of the daily experience of a new reading public. German-language papers took up the practice later on, notably Vienna's *Neue Freie Presse*. But it was in the age of the railroads, from the 1840s in England and a decade later on the continent, that publishing assumed modern forms and proportions. The book dealer W. H. Smith was already selling books in train stations in the 1840s (as the firm still does), and the larger and faster distribution networks that the new transport made possible replaced the old system of traveling sellers (*colporteurs* in France) with direct deliveries to town and village shops. Publicity for books expanded and prices fell; whereas a typical novel had an edition of around 1,000 copies before 1850, Jules Verne's self-consciously modern fictions appeared in runs of 30,000 in the 1870s, selling 1.6 million copies by 1904. Literature's presence in everyday life was further expanded by the new institution of the lending library.

These quantitative changes were accompanied by an important qualitative one. Literary relations before the nineteenth century were often of a personal, face-to face sort, declared in the fulsome dedications to their patrons that authors regularly offered in their books. Such effusions were testimony to the unavoidable dependence of writers on the direct material support of princes and aristocrats in a world not yet possessed of organized literary markets. Parallel relations existed between readers and literature, since booksellers often served a clientèle of people directly known to them, and to whom they provided individualized information about new publications. All these forms of literary life receded as the developments just noted proceeded. Writers began to rely on a wider, more anonymous public, made up of individuals who found access to literature in more impersonal ways, such as advertisements and newspaper reviews.

A similar trajectory marked the history of the visual arts. Not only were eighteenth-century painters and sculptors largely dependent upon private patrons in the same way as writers, collections of their work were essentially private spaces, too, located in the houses or palaces of the great, and open only to those who could make themselves known to the owners. The increased concern for public education during the self-proclaimed Age of Enlightenment encouraged some of these to transform their private storehouses into public venues. The British Museum, based on the objects assembled by a wealthy physician, Sir Hans Sloane, opened to the public in 1759; the Elector of Saxony invited his subjects to view his picture collection in a renovated Dresden stable in 1746; and the Habsburg emperor Joseph II dedicated the Belvedere Palace to a similar aim in 1770. The Uffizi in Florence and the Vatican in Rome both became public museums in 1775. But the history of such facilities reached a new stage with the opening of the Louvre as a museum by the French Revolutionary government in 1793, seeking to provide at once a demonstration of state support for culture and a place where the nation as a whole could be nurtured and "regenerated" by the great treasures of the human past (some of them in subsequent years brought to Paris by Napoleon's armies).

Similar ambitions were associated with the great expansion of the system of official painting Salons in France, where prizes and the éclat of official recognition brought living artists before a wide audience. The Salons became objects of sharp criticism from around the middle of the century, however, in part because the number of submissions mushroomed with the growing ranks of artists, leading to an expanding number of rejections, often on grounds denounced as arbitrary and regressive. Some of those rejected organized a famous "Salon des refusés" in 1863, part of a larger movement by painters and their friends to bypass the official system of the state and appeal directly to the public.

A crucial moment in this turn occurred with the emergence of the Impressionists in the 1870s. Although some of them continued to see the official Salons as necessary vehicles for reaching their audience, their public prominence owed much to the innovative system for bypassing the Salons that was devised by Paul Durand-Ruel, their chief dealer. Durand-Ruel more or less invented the modern practice of gallery exhibitions accompanied by catalogues that specified the virtues of the artists and objects displayed, supported by critics and periodicals. The purpose was not only to appeal directly to the public, but also to seek to form its taste, so as to bring both artists and buyers into a market free of influence by the merely wealthy or powerful. Although we commonly think of commercialism today as a threat to artistic independence and integrity, a number of innovative nineteenth-century artists and critics saw the immediate relationship to the public that market relations opened up as freeing them from dependence on overly powerful patrons, whether state or private. Durand-Ruel's system was an important inspiration for the so-called Secession movements of the fin-de-siècle, with the dealer Paul Cassirer closely imitating him in Berlin, and the painter Gustav Klimt involved with his counterparts in Vienna.

Like museums, public concerts (as opposed to private occasions in the homes of well-off patrons) were largely a creation of the eighteenth century, achieving prominence especially in England, where they often featured foreign luminaries such as Handel and Haydn. But their numbers mushroomed only later, increasing threefold in London between the mid 1830s and the late '40s and fivefold in Paris in the same years. In 1828 the soon-to-be-deposed Restoration government provided money for a Concert Society associated with the Paris Conservatory, thereby instituting what the *Journal des débats* called "a musical revolution." A slower growth was visible in Vienna, as in some smaller German cities, where *Kenner* and *Liebhaber*—knowers and lovers—organized public concerts, and in some capitals where princely theaters previously attended only by courtiers and their guests were opened to the public. These developments laid the foundation for the even more expanded audience for music that would exist by the end of the century, a counterpart to the expanded public for literature and the visual arts.

In this period, however, even public venues retained features rooted in private patronage. In Paris and London the most common kind of public concerts were dubbed "benefits," a term that did not mean an event held in aid of some outside cause, but one put on to support the musician who organized it. He (occasionally she, but mostly for singers) solicited colleagues to participate, and used the occasion less to profit from ticket sales than to put his name before potential patrons who could provide "more lucrative private concerts and teaching contracts," still the best source of income for most performers. Although such wildly popular traveling virtuosos as Niccolò Paganini and Franz Liszt did garner large sums from ticket sales, their tours were organized (like those of earlier figures such as Mozart) by the musicians themselves, through contacts with local patrons and colleagues, sometimes supported by aides whose relations to the soloists resembled servants more than later managers. Frédéric Chopin's career was even closer to the earlier model, since he gave few public concerts, and "lived on his earnings as a teacher with an extensive practice among the wealthy, [and] by his performances at the private concerts of the rich." The chief novel element in his case was the income he derived from publishing his works.

Within a few decades, however, a different and more recognizably modern concert regime emerged. Performers and composers ceased to be the main promoters of their own appearances, as professional managers and agents came on the scene from the 1870s, spreading to many cities in the next decades and creating relations between players and their audiences, much like those that Durand-Ruel and his imitators did for painters. "By 1900," as William Weber notes (the words quoted in the preceding paragraph are his too), "almost every concert program in London, Paris, Berlin, or Vienna denoted the concert agency that had arranged it."

A second aspect of the more public and palpable nature of musical life was the remarkable expansion of publishing. According to one report, there were only a dozen music shops in London around 1750, but 150 of them by 1824; between the same dates, catalogues of available pieces exploded from a few pages to several hundred, and by the 1820s the publisher Boosey (today Boosey & Hawkes) listed ten thousand pieces from foreign printing houses alone. In 1834 a multivolume "Musical Library" made its appearance in London, the publisher explaining that it was intended "to afford the same aid in the progress of the musical art that literature has so undeniably received from the cheap publications of the day." Teaching aids were one significant component of this output, along with collections of songs and instrumental pieces, especially for the pianos that found their way into more and more middle-class homes from late in the eighteenth century. All of these changes underlay a phenomenon Carl Dahlhaus identifies as giving a new cast to the situation of music in the nineteenth century, namely the emerging sense of a stable past repertoire against which new works could be compared and judged.

The expansion of literary publishing and the appearance of new and more public venues for the visual arts and music that began in the eighteenth century and accelerated in the nineteenth also contributed to endowing cultural practices and products with new meanings. Before 1800, most literate and educated Europeans continued to regard writers and artists of all kinds as best fulfilling their roles when their work served "higher" values or pursuits: overarching religious ideas and institutions, moral instruction, or courtly and aristocratic ceremonies and rituals. Viewed within the larger and more independent spaces they now occupied, however, cultural practices and objects came increasingly to be seen as constituting a distinct aesthetic sphere, identified by M. H. Abrams as the domain of "art as such," where they were expected to be judged on their own terms.

The philosopher Immanuel Kant gave theoretical support to this autonomy, arguing that what makes an object beautiful is that it fulfills its own purpose as fully as can be imagined, regardless of its possible relationship to anything outside itself. Kant famously described the best artists as people of "genius," a quality that at once freed them from subjection to existing rules and made them capable of stamping their creations with a deep unity and integrity that flowed from their own natures. The critic W. H. Wackenröder proposed that "galleries become 'temples' where, in silent humility and in heart-raising seclusion, one could take pleasure in marveling at the greatest artists as the highest of earthly beings." In music particularly such ideas contributed to the increased emphasis that Lydia Goehr has highlighted on compositions as "works" in an emphatic sense, integrated and self-regulating entities, all of whose parts contribute to the inner coherence of the whole. No cultural figure was more widely seen as producing such works of genius than Beethoven.

But culture's heightened autonomy generated worry and anxiety alongside these high titles. Freed of guidance by recognized moral or social authorities, both producers and consumers of culture displayed a potential to descend into a perilous realm of privacy. Painters and poets given space to make art on the basis of their own feelings often lived irregular and undisciplined "bohemian" lives, seemingly indifferent to traditional morality. The fact that readers, and especially young women, imbibed fictional stories alone and in private, unsupervised by parents, teachers, priests, or others able to provide proper direction, generated fantasies of moral abandon (famously dramatized by Gustave Flaubert in *Madame Bovary*).

As recent historians have shown, these sometimes lurid vexations—later to reappear in regard to movies, television, and the Internet—were important elements in the near panic that spread from late in the eighteenth century over masturbation. Long condemned but seldom obsessed over, solitary sex now became a widespread and disturbing preoccupation, imagined to cause all sorts of moral and physical disorders (now more or less universally regarded as imaginary). The anxiety was fed by fears about how far individuals might take their expanding opportunities for self-centered behavior in an age when many communal values and safeguards were losing their force, slipping, as Goethe put it, "into the seductive allurements of uncontrolled fancy." In this context, Thomas Laqueur concludes, masturbation loomed up as "the vice of individuation for a world in which the old ramparts against desire had crumbled," the exemplary evil of "an age that valued desire, pleasure, and privacy but was fundamentally worried about how, or if, society could mobilize them." The new shape of culture was deeply implicated in these worries.

What drew music into these anxieties was its nature as "the pure language of the passions," its special ability to represent and call forth feeling at its most elemental level. Speaking especially of Beethoven, George Sand wrote to Liszt that music "gives birth to feelings and ideas" lodged in "the most intimate depths of the self," evoking "everything you have felt, experienced, your loves, your suffering, your dreams," and throwing the listener "into an infinite reverie."

The possibility of experiencing music in this way was heightened by an exemplary feature of the changing settings in which it was heard, namely the turn to listening in silence. Music venues before the nineteenth century were hardly tranquil places. Treated by many as primarily social events, concerts and performances were the scene of often noisy interplay and conversation between audience members, and of a kind of social theater that dramatized the deference accorded to the socially most prominent among them. Etiquette books warned people not to express any reaction or opinion before some nearby "person of quality" had a chance to do so. The campaign for more attentive and involved audience behavior began early in the century, although it did not fully triumph until near the end. Critics and devotees, along with performers and conductors, all contributed to it, aiming to free the art they loved from the aristocratic dominance of social and cultural life that had long reigned. One result was to advance the notion of music as an autonomous realm, home to works of genius whose integrity and coherence were to be experienced in their own terms. At the same time, as a number of observers remarked, it encouraged individuals to value and express their individual reactions to what they heard in ways hindered by the earlier settings.

One account of what such listening could entail, fictional and idealized but resonant, at least, with widespread aspirations, and in some degree experiences, too, was penned by Wackenröder, the critic who proposed that museums become "temples."

> When Joseph was at a grand concert he seated himself in a corner, without so much as glancing at the brilliant assembly of listeners, and listened with precisely the same reverence as if he were in church—just as still and motionless, his eyes cast down to the floor. Not the slightest sound escaped his notice, and his keen attention left him in the end quite limp and exhausted.

Various elements were present in this portrayal. We will return in a moment to one of them, what Carl Dahlhaus calls "structured listening," the focused attention through which a hearer seeks "silently [to] retrace the act of composition" and thus to partake of the mental processes by which the composer achieved unity in a "work." But Joseph's experience was no less emotional than intellectual, and it is hard to miss the possible sexual overtone in his being left "in the end quite limp and exhausted." Music's power to draw listeners "downward" toward sensuality as well as "upward" toward contemplation and understanding had long been recognized, in the classical and Renaissance opposition between "noble" (usually string) and "base" (often wind) music. Echoes of this distinction appear in the nineteenth century, for instance in Felix Mendelssohn's often expressed "mistrust of sensual, 'materialistic' music that produced titillation of the senses rather than elevation and discipline of the feelings" (John Toews). Peter Gay suggests that music's potential to affect listeners in troubling ways was one reason for the appeal of silent listening: to demand mute attention of those with whom one shared a musical experience was not a snobbish disapproval of others who boorishly let their feelings hang out, but a protective reaction against the possibility of "a deeply regressive communion with one's [psychic and unconscious] past." There is no escaping the frank sexuality Richard Wagner wrote into some of his works, above all *Tristan and Isolde*.

The explicitly masturbatory potential in such sensuality was seldom acknowledged, but it is hard to miss in Thomas Mann's description of the pleasure that the teenage Hanno, the last member of the Buddenbrook family (sickly, he would not survive into manhood), took in the piano playing whose power to absorb him was a sign of his inability to participate in the practical ethic of worldly achievement exemplified by his forbears. Hanno delighted in the equivocal moments when harmonies were suspended between expectation and resolution, finding in them "the delight of sweet rapture . . . insistent, urgent longing," a sustained intimation of the happiness that "lasts only a moment." When he tells his friend Kai that in solitary moments he could not hold himself back from improvising, instead of practicing studies and sonatas as he should, descending into the realm of unfettered imagination and desire that it opened up (and that Goethe, as we saw, feared), Mann describes the sequel as follows:

> "I know what you're thinking when you improvise," Kai said. And then neither of them spoke.

> They were at a difficult age. Kai had turned beet-red and was staring at the ground, but without lowering his head. Hanno looked pale and very serious; he kept casting Kai enigmatic, sidelong glances.

Mann's vignette is testimony to his often pained awareness that the life of culture to which he was devoted brought dangers along with its benefits.

But the benefits were at least as substantial as the dangers, which brings us back to the "structured listening" to which Wackenröder's "Joseph" was devoted. Of all the arts, music is the one in which the heightening of private and sensual experience is most deeply linked up with the simultaneous generation of new possibilities for both intellectual understanding and social participation. This is precisely the summary view of what music meant to its nineteenth-century devotees, or at least the most involved and attentive of them, as offered by Gunilla Budde, a recent German historian of middle-class life.

> Music was understood by the nineteenth-century concert public not primarily as a mirror of reality, but as an autonomous world with its own structures, themes, forms of order, and encodings, one that required a high level of knowledge and analytical understanding for an adequate response, and which thereby fostered a communal and unifying potential for achieving such a response. At the same time, however, it provided room for freedom of personal experience and elaboration, whereby the subjectively variable "emotional chaos," subdued by the formal laws of harmony and rhythm, was transformed into an extensively individual version of "cosmic order." More than any other genre of high culture, concerts and operas made it possible to gather the feelings of individuals at a single place and time together in a shared experience of artistic pleasure.

If Budde is right—and her account is based on wide reading in memoirs, letters, and commentary—then music provided a point of interchange at once between feeling and intellect, and between deeply private and strongly social involvements and connections. Perhaps more than any other art, music brought people face to face with both the threat and the promise of culture in its new and more modern shape.

Alexander Borodin the Composer

PETER LAKI

Throughout his all-too-short life, Alexander Borodin (1833–1887) was keenly aware of the Russian proverb according to which "if you chase two hares, you will catch neither." Borodin's two hares were his two loves, music and chemistry—and as one of the leading Russian chemists and one of the most important Russian composers of his time, he proved the proverb wrong.*

The two aspects of Borodin's remarkable dual career unfolded side by side, and at no point did he neglect one field for the other. As a child, he took piano lessons and played the flute; his principal instrument, however, was the cello, on which he became quite proficient. His main ambition, meanwhile, was a career in science, and at the age of 17, he enrolled at the St. Petersburg Medical-Surgical Academy, where he earned a medical degree eight years later. Even during his medical studies, he was an active amateur musician, frequently playing his cello at private chamber-music gatherings. During his student years he met a young cadet named Modest Mussorgsky, with whom he shared a love of music. They didn't become friends at that time because as soon as Borodin graduated from the Academy, he went to Europe for three years of further training in chemistry.

After his return to St. Petersburg in 1862, Borodin, now 29 years old, was introduced to Mily Balakirev by one of his colleagues at the Medical-Surgical Academy, a young doctor named Sergey Botkin, who was also an amateur cellist. Balakirev, a composer and pianist four years younger than Borodin, was already mentor to a group of amateur composers. The group, whose members included Mussorgsky, Nikolai Rimsky-Korsakov, and Cesar Cui, eventually became known as the "Mighty Handful," or, after Borodin joined, the "Russian Five." Borodin, entirely self-taught as

*Borodin's accomplishments as a chemist are described in "Alexander Borodin the Chemist" by Swapan S. Jain, page 101 of this volume.

a composer, had already written several chamber works (some of them unfinished), including a string quintet with two cellos, a piano trio, a string trio (two violins and cello), a cello sonata, and a piano quintet. These works, unpublished until many years after Borodin's death, bear witness to his extraordinary facility, rich melodic invention, and sure command of form even at this early stage. Having seen some of these scores, Balakirev convinced the young chemist to take composition more seriously and encouraged him to try his hand at a symphony. Further inspiration came from Borodin's wife, Katya, an accomplished pianist.

Due to his many professional commitments, Borodin needed more than five years to complete his symphony. After Balakirev's appointment as conductor of the Russian Music Society, he led the symphony's public premiere in 1869. Although the performance was poor, due to the sloppily prepared orchestral parts, it marked an auspicious professional debut for Borodin who, from now on, fully embraced composition as his second career. The symphony itself succeeded and later made a strong impression on Franz Liszt, who became one of Borodin's strongest supporters on the international scene.

As a true member of the "Mighty Handful," who were intent on developing in music an authentic Russian style independent from German models, Borodin knew that he had to write an opera on a Russian historical subject. Mussorgsky had already started work on *Boris Godunov*, and Rimsky-Korsakov on *Maid of Pskov*.

Borodin based his opera on *The Tale of Igor's Campaign*, a medieval Russian epic. The topic was suggested to him by the critic Vladimir Stasov, who had an enormous influence on all aspects of Russian cultural life in the 19th century. Borodin worked on his opera, *Prince Igor*, for the rest of his life, during whatever spare time he had. Due to his multiple responsibilities as a researcher and chemistry professor, however, the opera remained unfinished at the time of his sudden death in 1887. For many years, *Prince Igor* was known as completed by Rimsky-Korsakov and Alexander Glazunov. In a striking departure from that version, the opera's recent revival at the Metropolitan Opera presented a form of the work closer to what Borodin had in mind. For the first time, audiences could hear a great deal of material written by Borodin that had been suppressed or neglected by the nineteenth-century editors.

The Tale of Igor's Campaign is about the war fought by Igor, a prince in Rus (the medieval precursor of modern Russia) against the Polovtsians (also known as Cumans), a nomadic tribe speaking a Turkic language that controlled vast territories from the Black Sea to the Caspian Sea and beyond. Stasov prepared a detailed scenario for Borodin to use, but the composer, who wrote his own libretto, made major changes to what he had been given.

The opera is best known for the colorful "Polovtsian Dances," often performed separately in concert, but just as impressive are the vast choruses sung by the Russian people. Choral scenes are centrally important in national opera, where their function is to represent the voice of the masses; yet this opera's chief glory undoubtedly lies in the writing for the soloists. *Prince Igor* has a relatively large cast, and each character is portrayed vividly in the music. The protagonist is a brave warrior who has been defeated, a loving husband and father whose son becomes a traitor; he at first resists the idea of escaping from Polovtsian captivity because he thinks it dishonorable to do so, but is finally persuaded to take flight in the interests of his country and to return to his wife, Yaroslavna.

Igor's opponent, Khan Konchak, is no wild barbarian but rather a noble enemy who regards Igor as a guest, not a prisoner; he proposes an alliance, but Igor rejects it. The women receive equally nuanced treatment. Yaroslavna laments her husband's absence but shows remarkable strength when the situation demands it. And Konchakovna, the Khan's daughter, who seduces Igor's son Vladimir, exudes unbridled sexuality, singing in a sultry contralto; she also deeply loves Vladimir and at one point declares that she is willing to die if that will save his life. Nor did Borodin forget the need for comic relief; he included a pair of drunken minstrels, Eroshka and Skula, whose parts are nevertheless integral to the plot.

The opera's chief villain is Prince Galitsky, Yaroslavna's brother, whom Igor put in charge of his affairs when he went to war. Galitsky's drinking song is one of the highlights of the opera, but his most prominent character trait is his brutal pursuit of women. When a group of village girls comes complaining to Yaroslavna that Galitsky has forcibly abducted and raped one of their friends, the Princess angrily confronts her brother, who gives her a chillingly cynical reply. In this scene (which was not in Stasov's scenario, let alone in the original poem), we recognize Borodin the staunch feminist, one of the early champions of women's education who taught at a school for midwives at a time when most women were barred from higher studies. The contrast between Galitsky's and Igor's characters is further emphasized when the latter refuses the slave girls that Konchak offers him in every quantity.

Even as he was toiling away at his opera, Borodin worked on numerous other compositional projects during the last decade or so of his life. His First Symphony was followed by a Second, which many regard as Borodin's instrumental masterpiece. He also composed a short symphonic poem entitled "In the Steppes of Central Asia," a number of fine songs and a seven-movement Miniature Suite for piano solo. In addition, he remained true to his early love of chamber music for strings, and composed two quartets (1875 and 1881) that are invaluable additions to the repertoire. The title page of the first quartet states that it was "inspired by a theme of Beethoven," and, in fact, the main theme of the first movement is taken from the finale of Beethoven's B-flat major quartet, Op. 130. Borodin combined this classical inspiration with other themes of a distinctly Russian flavor, some of them related to themes from the opera.

The second quartet contains a "Notturno" that became perhaps the most famous of all of Borodin's melodies. At one time, it was popular in the United States with the lyric "And This Is My Beloved" from the 1953 musical *Kismet*, all made up of adaptions of Borodin's music. The musical also contained a tune from the Polovtsvian Dances rewritten as "Stranger in Paradise." Even in its original form, it is practically a love song, or, rather, a love duet between the first violin and the cello.

Over the years, Borodin's First Symphony became an international success that led to his growing fame in Western Europe and won him the friendship of an influential countess in Belgium and, through her, many other important contacts abroad. In the 1880s, he was fêted as a composer in Germany, France, and Belgium; but whenever he was back in Russia, he continued his scientific research and teaching. All of these demands (to which we must add his wife's precarious state of health, a constant source of worry and aggravation) eventually took a toll. A serious heart condition was diagnosed late in 1886 but went untreated; the night of February 27, 1887, Borodin collapsed at a party and died instantly of a massive heart attack, at the age of 53. Katya survived him by only a few months.

After Borodin's death, Rimsky-Korsakov and Glazunov took it upon themselves to complete and publish the unfinished works. In addition to their work on *Prince Igor*, Glazunov also completed Borodin's Third Symphony, and Rimsky-Korsakov edited Borodin's contributions to an earlier, aborted opera-ballet project called *Mlada*, a collaborative effort involving Mussorgsky, Rimsky-Korsakov, Borodin, and Cui. When *Prince Igor* finally reached the stage in 1890, audiences received it enthusiastically. (The bass Fyodor Stravinsky, whose soon-to-be-famous son was named after the opera's protagonist, sang the role of the minstrel Skula.)

Because of his dual career, the catalogue of Borodin's works is not extensive; yet the world of Russian music was never the same after him. Stasov put it beautifully in a letter to the painter Ilya Repin, written on October 20, 1887, after listening to Borodin's music at a rehearsal: "What a colossus, what grandiosity, what strength, what beauty, what passion, what magic! I had tears in my eyes the entire time. There has been no one like that since Glinka. He was the brother of our poor Mussorgsky, he was like a lion."

Alexander Borodin the Chemist

BY SWAPAN S. JAIN

Alexander P. Borodin made significant contributions in the field of organic chemistry even though he did not receive any formal training in the subject. Borodin's training in medicine at the St. Petersburg Medical-Surgical Academy included courses in chemistry in which he took a special interest, learning, apparently, through a process of trial and error. The Chemistry Department at the Academy was chaired by Professor Nikolay Zinin, who served as Borodin's mentor—a relationship that has been characterized as paternal—in both professional and personal pursuits. Zinin made significant contributions to the nascent field of organic chemistry, including the Zinin reduction reaction of nitrobenzene to aniline (aniline is used to make a variety of household and industrial goods such as rubber, pesticides, explosives, and pharmaceutical agents). Zinin was also the chemistry teacher of Alfred Nobel, who established the Nobel Prize.

In his third year of medical training, Borodin made a formal request to work in Zinin's chemistry laboratories. Such a request was uncommon, as medical students rarely ventured outside the field of medicine to conduct research under a mentor. Borodin's pursuits are akin to a path pursued by modern day MD-PhD dual-degree students in the United States.

During Borodin's medical and research training, Zinin advised him to look for advanced training and experience in Western Europe, where fine chemicals, equipment, and laboratory resources were more readily available. Heidelberg was a favorite destination for many Russian chemists. Borodin left for Heidelberg in November 1859, sent by the Academy, for three years with full salary and an extra allowance of 1,000 silver rubles. He wrote to his mother that he was not going to Western Europe for a pleasure trip but as an individual commissioned for the purpose of "attaining perfection in science." After some failed attempts at finding an appropriate place to work, Borodin was provided with a private room in

Portrait of the Composer and Scientist Alexander Borodin by Ilya Repin, 1888
State Russian Museum, St. Petersburg, Russia. Bridgeman Images

Erlenmeyer Flask. Photo by Swapan S. Jain in the Bard College chemistry laboratories.

the laboratory of Emil Erlenmeyer. There Borodin received fine specialty chemicals from Merck, then a relatively small pharmaceutical corporation.

Erlenmeyer made enormous contributions in the field of organic chemistry. Working primarily as a theoretical chemist, he developed rules that were essential to understanding the oxidation of aldehydes and ketones (molecules containing a carbon double-bonded to an oxygen, $C=O$). Oxidation reactions involve the addition of oxygen to an existing substance. They are widespread not only inside human cells during the breakdown of food but also in industrial applications such as the rusting of iron and combustion of fuels. The Erlenmeyer flask, found in every chemistry lab around the world, is named for Emil Erlenmeyer.

Erlenmeyer worked under another prominent organic chemist, August Kekulé, who founded the theory of chemical structure. Kekulé's most important contribution is likely the elucidation of the ring structure of benzene (page 103). The benzene molecule is a scaffold for thousands of other organic compounds that occur naturally and are produced synthetically in the laboratory. Kekulé proposed that benzene was a six-member ring of carbon atoms with alternating single and double bonds.

While working in Erlenmeyer's laboratories in Heidelberg, Borodin started his investigations as an organic chemist into the reaction of

Chemical structure of benzene, constructed using ChemDraw 13.0 software.

Rearrangement of benzidine, illustrated using ChemDraw 13.0 software.

benzidines. Note that there are two benzene rings in each structure shown on the left and the right side of the arrow in the illustration. One of Borodin's important contributions to the field of organic chemistry was the elucidation of the reaction mechanism of benzidine rearrangement. Benzidines are used to make a variety of dyes in the chemical industry today.

Borodin abandoned the topic of benzidines, however, after learning that August Wilhelm von Hoffman, a distinguished chemist and an academic with enormous experience and access to resources, was also working in the same area. Borodin was wise to focus his energy elsewhere because Hoffman published the first paper on benzidines in 1860.

One of Borodin's good friends, Dmitri I. Mendeleyev, was the Russian chemist credited with the discovery of the periodic table of elements, regarded as one of the most important contributions to modern science. Borodin spent considerable time in Mendeleyev's company, in Russia and in Western Europe. Borodin was usually short of money and often asked his friend Dmitri for help. Borodin's adventures, it seems, were not limited to chemistry and music.

In September 1860, the first International Chemical Congress (ICC) took place in Karlsruhe, Germany. This seminal event in the history of

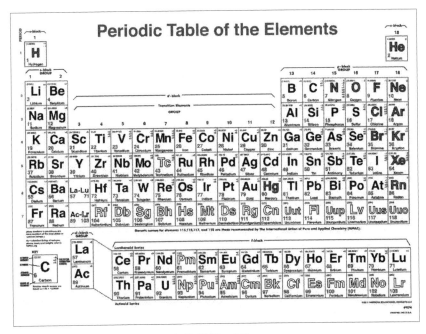

Periodic Table of Elements

chemistry was attended by 140 participants, including well-known chemists like Mendeleyev, Erlenmeyer, Zinin, Kekulé, and Charles-Adolph Wurtz, and also the young Alexander Borodin. The purpose of the conference was to reach agreement and consensus on fundamental issues of importance in chemistry. In those days, the dissemination of data and research results obtained by individuals the world over was very challenging. The cornerstone of modern research is peer review and critique by fellow scientists in the field. Advances in technology, transportation, and availability of resources have made the peer-review process much easier than it was during the 1800s, when meetings such as the ICC provided, every few years, perhaps the only opportunity for scientists to reach agreement and conclusions on common topics of scientific inquiry. At that first meeting of the ICC, for example, the consequences of the difference between atoms and molecules were discussed. Although Borodin was not mentioned in the formal reports and papers of that first ICC, he was fortunate to have been invited, as he was able to make contact with prominent scientists.

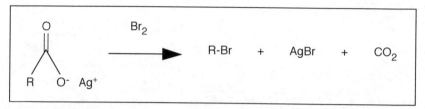

Borodin-Hunsdiecker Reaction, illustrated using ChemDraw 13.0 software.

After the ICC, Borodin continued his research in Heidelberg. He described the reaction of silver carboxylate salts (shown on the left side of the arrow in the figure above) with liquid bromine, Br_2. This is an example of a halogenation reaction, in which carbon dioxide is removed as a product along with silver bromide salt. This reaction can be used to synthesize bromine-containing compounds. Brominated compounds are commonly used as pesticides and disinfectants.

In 1861 Borodin traveled to Paris and presented this work in a session of *Société Chimique*. The following year, he published the work in Germany. Many decades later, this reaction was rediscovered by Heinz and Clare Hunsdiecker and patented in 1935. Almost every organic chemist knows this reaction as the Hunsdiecker reaction, despite Borodin's earlier discovery. Today it is correctly named the Borodin-Hunsdiecker reaction.

During his work in Pisa, Borodin was able to transform benzoyl chloride (shown on the left in the figure on page 106) to benzoyl fluoride using a platinum vessel, which likely acted as a catalyst for this reaction. Benzoyl fluoride was the third organic fluorine compound ever prepared and the first prepared by substituting fluorine (F) for chlorine (Cl). Today, an entire division of the American Chemical Society (an association of more than 120,000 scientists around the world) investigates fluorine-based compounds. Fluorinated molecules are extremely valuable in the pharmaceutical industry. For instance, fluoroquinolones are an important class of fluorine containing antibiotics that are prescribed today. Lipitor (a cholesterol-lowering drug) also contains fluorine. Other fluorinated medicinal agents include those that function as antihistamines, antacids, antimalarials, and antidepressants.

Borodin returned to Saint Petersburg in 1863, promised a professorship in organic chemistry as well as a new research laboratory at the Medical-Surgical Academy. This promise took two years to come true; in the meantime, Borodin was appointed an adjunct professor and given access to one of Professor Zinin's old laboratories. Borodin's annual salary

Platinum catalyzed synthesis of benzoyl fluoride,
illustrated using ChemDraw 13.0 software.

Structure of an Aldol molecule, created using ChemDraw 13.0 software.

at the time was a mere 700 rubles, as he wrote in frustration to his friend Alexander Butlerov. For this Borodin supervised laboratory experiments, delivered the occasional lecture, and held examinations. In 1865, the Academy finally appointed him full professor of organic chemistry.

Borodin continued to work in his laboratory at the Academy. His greatest accomplishment as an organic chemist was to discover, along with Charles-Adolphe Wurtz, a reaction, known as Aldol Condensation, in which two molecules are joined into one. Bond formation reactions between two carbon atoms (C-C) are very challenging to conduct but have a high impact in the field of synthesis and the development of new compounds.

In addition to his work as a musician and a chemist, Borodin was a champion of women's education in science and medicine. He gave women many opportunities for training as scientists in his laboratory, and was a founder of the School of Medicine for Women in Saint Petersburg. His sudden death in 1887 cut short a career that would have been remarkable in either field alone, chemistry or music. The world is fortunate that he pursued both.

REFERENCE

William G. Vijvers, *Alexander Borodin: Composer, Scientist, Educator*. (Amsterdam: The American Book Center, 2013).

Some Matters of Music and Poetry

ROBERT KELLY

Every child knows it. Hears human voices singing and the orchestra making sounds, hears one voice lifted out from others, singing a tune.

"What is he saying?" the child asks.

There are operas I have listened to a dozen times without bothering my head about what he is "saying," that purring Fischer-Dieskau or radiant Corelli. Janáček's *From the House of the Dead* I first heard, and many times heard, on a borrowed unlabeled tape—heard it dozens of times before I even learned what it was (though it clearly sounded like Janáček). What was wrong with me, that I took such delight in a plotless, wordless opera, where the shouted and chanted Czech was just more wonderful sound?

But I knew the true story of that opera. It wasn't what Janáček had in mind, wasn't the Dostoevsky novella, wasn't Siberia. It was its own story, a story told exclusively by the sounds. It was the story Janáček's genius compelled or permitted him to tell, the "real" story of the opera. The story that happens in the head of the ignorant but fascinated listener.

I was a heretic. I came for the music.

Aristotle was perhaps wrong to downgrade *opsis*, spectacle, in his hierarchy of dramatic values. Nowadays opera seems to be sold as spectacle, presumably to an audience equally charmed by Adams as by Monteverdi as long as it's given something "sumptuous" to behold. Personally, I think of this as the Barnum and Bailey approach to opera.

Wait, enough of my heresies.

I am a writer; for and in my own practice, words are all-important. To be true to the words, their geneses, their currencies, sounds, shades, nuances, to listen to the words and follow where they lead me—that's the essence of my practice.

When the words come to a composer, let them come in the same way—let them lead to sounds, let sentences lead to song, the urgent paragraph or stanza lead to aria.

Let the words die into the music.

A poem never truly lives till it dies into the reader's sensorium, into the music, into the truly heard. That's the core of what I'm saying here.

Heraclitus left us a haunting fragment: *dying each other's life, living each other's death.*

And that is the relation that compels poetry in opera—the words beget the music and die into it, music fades away and leaves the words as tunes or tones or just some sense behind it.

And of course from music comes poetry, the unknown but vast number of poems that "come from" rapt hearing of Chopin, Beethoven, Biber, Mahler, Palestrina, no music that has not cast its spell on poetry. I don't talk about it here because it's so obvious. Sometimes I think I would be silenced without music.

But that's music in general, and my sights at the minute are fixed on opera.

I've been impressed for years by the difference between song and opera, which offhand would seem much the same.

In a way, song is the very opposite of opera.

The greatest writer of lieder in our canon, Schubert, left dozens and dozens of songs (Think of "The Linden Tree," "The Hurdy-gurdy Man") where every syllable is distinct, and hearing the words is as easy, and important, as if the singer were speaking them to you alone. In fact, that privacy, the me-to-thee quality, is essential in Schubert.

But that is not the way of opera. Even Schubert's opera. Poem vanishes into song, the words take wing, their vocalic cores spread wide, their consonants chipped away. And it is interesting that from the first centuries of opera down through Puccini, when words have to be understood if the drama is to be grasped at all, they're produced as recitative or outright spoken ("before him, all Rome trembled.")

I'm not saying that lexical incomprehensibility is the essence of opera—just think of the catalogue aria in *Don Giovanni*, or Baron Ochs's self-consolings in *Rosenkavalier*, where we get every word, and the punch lines ring out. If you happen to know Italian. If you happen to know German. If you happen, in other words, not to be an ordinary listener, for whom *keine Nacht dir zu lang* is just a drunk passing out on his way down to low F.

I think about Wilhelm Müller, whose poems we never read in German class. Whose poems Schubert took and made immortal, unmasking the eternity hidden between the lines. The lines were doorways, and he went through. Bringing us with him.

I can't remember offhand the name of the Belgian fin-de-siècle poet whose words Schönberg transfigured in *Pierrot Lunaire*. His settings of those texts are remarkable critical acts in themselves, the way the poems are changed, compressed, made powerful by the curious fact that much of the text gets banished into regions of the voice where we can't follow, are there *sous-rature* so to speak, while what we can discern takes on power not just from the vocalism it allows, but in the way the music focuses our attention on words that *do* stand up to thoughtful hearing.

Strauss had the good fortune to work intensely and interestingly for years with a very good poet indeed, Hugo von Hofmannsthal, whose work we did indeed read in German class (and whose "Lord Chandos' Letter" is a Modernist masterpiece too little known hereabouts). But even that remarkable poet's verse tended, and rightly so, to shimmer, to vanish into the ardent moonlight of Strauss's music—think of the trio and duet that conclude *Rosenkavalier*, the most exalted music ever committed to women's voices after Bellini. After the Marschalin's half-spoken beginning, who cares, who dares, to interrupt the sublimity of those sounds in search of some verbal approximation of what those women are feeling, deciding, avowing? The music tells us all.

Alas for opera when it talks and forgets to sing, where interminable recitative replaces the rich entanglement of voices in their differences, their interplay with orchestral sounds. Alas for a culture where opera seeks to be relevant instead of being the gnomon against which relevance is measured. Or where opera carouses in opulence or grows sanctimonious with austerity.

Wagner is misread by those who think that the gradual disappearance of aria-singing in his later work intended the death of melody. His leitmotivs, dozens of them in the *Ring*, in *Parsifal*, are themselves melodies, tiny arias, and those efficient melodies, alone or in ever-changing combinations, transformation, bring a ceaseless flow of song. *Endlose Melodie*, Wagner demanded, not merely endless sound.

Let's try to help current opera overcome its aesthetic timidity, overcome its fear of the aria as being old-fashioned, unnatural—as if opera weren't the most unnatural art west of Kabuki. Fleeing aria, some make the fatal blunder of fleeing melody with it—leaving not just opera but musical theater in general impoverished, given a little spasmodic life by rhythm and spectacle alone.

A poet thinks: if all goes well, maybe some of my words (words themselves, how dare I call them mine) will die into music. That's what I would call really living.

Building for Music

DEBORAH BERKE

The usually private, closed-door practice studios were on display during the opening dedication of the László Z. Bitó '60 Conservatory Building at the Bard College Conservatory of Music. Visitors could stand in the doorway of one room and watch musicians playing string instruments, then move down the hall and hear flute, piano, or horns. Classical music, early music, and student compositions were offered in an experience similar to browsing the stalls of the open-air markets of Barcelona or Paris and being struck by an extravaganza, not of delectable goods, but of delicious sounds.

Afterward, we sat on upholstered metal chairs in the performance space to hear a poem written for the occasion, a moving tribute by the college president, and an inspirational speech by the building's donor. Then the speaker's lectern was turned around to serve the needs of a conductor, who led a small student orchestra in producing sounds that filled the room and enveloped all my senses. As the architect of the building, I was particularly thrilled to see the room used in so many different ways on its first day.

As I listened to the music, I thought about how crucial public presentation—be it a poetry reading, jazz concert, dance performance, or sculpture exhibition—is to the teaching of the arts. Students need the audience interaction as rite of passage in their education and, perhaps more important, as an introduction to the reciprocity cycle of creative process: you make work in private, incubating something away from judgment; share that work in public and receive feedback in the form of applause, reviews, money, or opportunities; and then take the experience back into the studio and make more work.

On my second visit to the conservatory, during regular school hours, I thought about this reciprocity again, but in terms of the need for solitude and isolation. The studio doors were all closed, giving privacy and focus to students practicing or receiving instruction. In the performance hall, a string group was rehearsing a classical piece with a piano. The sound in the space was just as stunning as it had been during the concert—bright and crisp—yet the arrangement of the room was informal and the musicians loose yet focused. It was akin to encountering ballet dancers in their leg warmers after seeing them in costume and on stage.

At the most basic level, then, a music school needs two kinds of spaces: small, cellular rooms for practice and isolation, and a larger room for performance. These specific requirements speak to significant and broad ideas about the give-and-take—a yin and yang of private and public—that exists in the way artists work. And this duality parallels my own process as an architect: you start alone; share what you're thinking with a small team; your team grows to include engineers and consultants; your design becomes a building; and occupants enjoy the finished space. You have shown the occupants ways to inhabit spaces that they had not previously considered, and they, in turn, discover ways to use the spaces that you had not imagined. The entire process informs your next design.

Architectural spaces for teaching the arts accommodate the pedagogical traditions attached to this cycle. Yet with a conservatory in particular, this reciprocity also contains a kind of generosity and sharing: there is a sense of "receiving" instruction and a "giving back" of what has been learned, to the public, to the audience.

Working from smallest to largest, the core spaces of the Bard conservatory include lockers, practice rooms, and the performance hall. The lockers come in four sizes: small (violin, viola, flute, oboe, clarinet, bassoon, trumpet, and trombone); medium (cello); medium-large (French horn); and large (bass and tuba). The lockers stand in single rows and never opposite one another: this prevents students from bumping into each other and their instruments during major rehearsal times or high-traffic moments of leaving school or going to practice. The corridors are wide enough for two students, each carrying a large instrument, to pass by other students loading or unloading their lockers.

In my mind's eye, the student comes in, takes her instrument (already in its own specialized case) out of a locker designed specifically for its shape and size, and then "unwraps" that instrument in one of the twelve practice rooms. These spaces themselves provide another kind

Sketch by Maitland Jones, of Deborah Berke Partners.

of specialized and protective shelter, and the entire building serves as a protective enclosure around all this activity.

Unlike rooms in a regular building, practice spaces do not share walls but instead have parallel separate walls. To control noise and vibration, the studios are designed like envelopes. The floor of each room flows up to form its own walls, which, along with the ceiling, are covered with acoustic surfaces that absorb and reflect sound. At Bard, the goal was for the rooms, despite their small size, to reproduce the sound a musician would hear when performing in a larger concert hall; this type of environment prepares students for a range of different venues in a way a typical practice booth cannot.

Materials also help create the feeling of a concert space. Wood floors transmit sound through a musician's feet, chair, and instrument. The gray fabrics of the acoustic panels balance the warm tones of the floor, and their texture recalls the wool and mohair of seating in traditional theaters.

All of the acoustic panels at Bard were off-the-shelf or semi-custom made, so our work involved arranging them for function and artistry. The paramount rule: No symmetry! Music sounds too loud when reflected directly back to the musician and too dull when played directly into absorption. We mixed different types and sizes of panels to create a harmonious pattern—asymmetrical yet not haphazard. Always composed.

In terms of the practice-room sizes, each is designed to house a medium-size or grand piano. One studio accommodates two grand pianos

Sketch by Maitland Jones, of Deborah Berke Partners.

side by side for the teaching of technique. (This was certainly our first experience designing a building with eighteen pianos.)

In contrast to the specific requirements of the practice rooms, the Bitó performance space is designed for complete spatial flexibility. It departs from the usual concert hall by having a flat open floor and no fixed stage location or fixed seats. It also has windows, providing daylight and glimpses of trees that acknowledge the seasons and times of day. Nothing in the space dictates the location of performers or audience. A single performer can play in a corner, or musicians can stand in a line. The audience could be positioned in many and unexpected configurations. Once students hone their skills in rooms tailored for the tradition of practice and instruction, they enter a nontraditional space of free creative expression. This is the crucial difference between the practice and performance spaces, aside from their scale. The red acoustic panels in the concert area signal the occasion of performance visually by being rich in color and texture. Hard painted surfaces reflect sound; soft wool-covered ones absorb it.

The idea within acoustics of sound's needing to be both reflected and absorbed to create a balance has a parallel in architecture. A similar kind of tuning happens in the way the spaces of a building recede or protrude into the field of vision. Externally, on the Bitó Conservatory Building, the brick walls of the performance space jut out to signal its location to an arriving audience, while its dark rich texture and color is understated. In contrast, the practice rooms are housed in a large white volume that curves away; it reflects light and attracts attention with its color and texture, yet retreats in its form, as if to suggest the need for isolation that drives the purpose of the rooms it contains.

Reflecting and absorbing, as balancing concepts, are not dissimilar to the give-and-take within learning, teaching, or practicing within a creative field. In learning, you absorb or internalize a skill and a tradition; in performing, you reflect back the results of that education. But learning continues beyond the conservatory in what the artist—or the architect— gains or "absorbs" from presenting her work to the public. The cycle of reciprocity continues. Your work as an architect doesn't end when you complete a project, just as your work as a musician doesn't end with the applause after a performance. You're back at it the next day, playing your instrument, painting your next canvas, sketching your next building.

"Nothing Is Too Good for the Working Class": Classical Music, the High Arts, and Workers' Culture[1]

JOHN HALLE

The New York Philharmonic's Henry Kravis Award, financed by a seven-figure withdrawal from the ten-figure bank account of one of America's more notorious financers, is one of many indications that while its influence has waned, classical music still has friends in high places. These connections tend to accrue mainly to high profile conductors, opera stars, and virtuoso soloists. But even those not inhabiting the peaks of the profession will occasionally find themselves recipients of scholarships, grants, or small awards for which plutocrats of various sorts have footed the bill. And so it is not uncommon to find ourselves at a dinner or reception where we, or friends of ours, are being feted, and, in this capacity, to shake the hand of a bona fide one-percenter, engaging in small talk with him (it is usually him) or, more likely, his spouse.

While it requires a substantial leap of imagination to see much of an overlap between our interests and theirs, musicians' comparatively close proximity to elites makes it understandable that we are more susceptible to the infection that the Marxists diagnose as false consciousness. Whether we are capable of identifying and acting politically in accordance with our real economic interests, as opposed to those of our aspirational or imagined social milieu, is the question raised in my article "Composers and the Plutocracy."[2] While I will have something more to say about that in the following, the main focus will be on a related, reciprocal question: whether the work that we and others produce in the so-called high arts has a place within a movement for the 99 percent.

Any discussion around this subject needs to begin with the recognition that for at least three generations now, the answer to the question has been an obvious *no*. The high arts generally, and classical music in particular, are seen as, if not by the elite, for them, which is to say designed mainly for their consumption and, as argued by Lawrence Levine,[3] serving their agenda. It will therefore seem farfetched to claim that classical music could serve as a medium for critiquing the 1 percent and function in support of mass movements.

But it turns out that in the not too distant past, many on the left took it for granted that music could do this. The main period where this potential was explored, namely, during the political and artistic ferment within what is known as the cultural front,[4] provides us not only inspiration, but also indications of how a movement in which we are involved might take shape and what our role within it might consist of. For this reason, it seems worth revisiting some of this history and the controversies that became inevitable as artists made a sincere effort to function in the service of the 99 percent, repudiating their traditional relationship with economic and social elites.

Of course, while granting the possibility that we can move from false to class consciousness, we need to concede that the well-worn stereotypes of classical musicians as mannered and obsequious servants of wealth and the wealthy are based on fact, albeit facts from three centuries ago. Then, as is well known, most composers were, like Haydn, attached to, or, like Mozart, failing to acquire positions within, European dynastic royal courts. Bach, at the beginning of his career, was also a beneficiary of these arrangements. A good indication of what was expected of him and the others in their relations with superiors was the composer's inscription on title page of the Brandenburg Concerti:

> As I had the good fortune a few years ago to be heard by Your Royal Highness, at Your Highness's commands, and as I noticed then that Your Highness took some pleasure in the little talents which Heaven has given me for Music, and as in taking Leave of Your Royal Highness, Your Highness deigned to honour me with the command to send Your Highness some pieces of my Composition: I have in accordance with Your Highness's most gracious orders taken the liberty of rendering my most humble duty to Your Royal Highness with the present Concertos, which I have adapted to several instruments; begging Your Highness most humbly not to judge their imperfection with the rigor of that

discriminating and sensitive taste, which everyone knows
Him to have for musical works, but rather to take into benign
Consideration the profound respect and the most humble
obedience which I thus attempt to show Him.

Bach's transparently absurd protestations of his "little talents" and
"imperfections" and his entreaties to be exempted from his majesty's stern
but fair judgment are a lavish albeit not atypical display of flattery, understood then not as demeaning to, but as required of, those expecting to
remain "in service." At the same time, musicians recognized their value to
the court and were sometimes able to negotiate favorable terms for their
service. But overly aggressive assertions of independence would subject
them to punishment, Mozart's disciplining at the hands of the Salzburg
Archbishop being the most celebrated instance; Bach having served a prison
term for incurring the displeasure of his royal patron in Dresden is another.

Aristocratic patronage remained a source of composers' livelihoods
throughout the nineteenth century, with Beethoven's annuity contract,
which supported him from 1809 until the end of his life, secured through
the contributions of a consortium of Viennese nobility. Later in the century, Tchaikovsky's musical career was lavishly supported in equal measure by the Imperial Court and by a generous allowance made available to him by his admirer, Madame von Meck, an heiress to a railway
fortune. Each of these arrangements, significantly, required very little
of either composer. Most notably, they did not require the composer's
appearance at court, or even his presence in the near vicinity: Beethoven
was required only to remain in Vienna; Tchaikovsky, famously, met his
patroness on only one occasion, their relationship having been otherwise
entirely epistolary. Independence, as opposed to subservience, was by
this point taken as the great artist's prerogative, and elites were willing
to underwrite financially the conditions necessary for artists to achieve it.

In this connection, it is hard to avoid mentioning the figure of Richard
Wagner, who parlayed musical genius, formidable intellect, and social
connections into a position of considerable economic power and political
influence.[5] While Wagner would be appropriated and serve as a foun-
dational inspiration for National Socialism, less well known is Wagner's
friendship with Bakunin and his leadership role in the 1849 Dresden
uprisings.[6] That Wagner would remain in the good graces of European
royals, ultimately being provided an unlimited budget by his Bayreuth
patron King Ludwig, is indicative of composers' relating to hereditary

nobility on an increasingly equal footing—recognized by the latter as de facto "aristocrats of the soul."

Roughly concurrent with these evolving forms of elite patronage was the ascendancy of the merchant class and the growth of cities, which led to the creation of large public concert halls where performances were highly lucrative for touring virtuosi. Fees derived from concerts were augmented by sales of composers' works through the burgeoning music publishing industry, and eventually, recordings, the combination of which provided some musicians access to real wealth. Eventually, musicians were increasingly able to cut their ties with feudal courts and patrons entirely, becoming entrepreneurs marketing and selling their musical product to an increasingly affluent consumer base.

But, having managed to thrive under the market's invisible hand, musicians found themselves increasingly subject to its vicissitudes. This became most apparent during the post–World War I period in which Europe was unable to regain its economic footing. By the 1930s, conditions had deteriorated to the point that many began to question elites' competence in managing economic affairs and their moral and intellectual fitness to govern. This recognition in some cases emboldened musicians to begin to question their traditional allegiance to the political right.[7] In this context we begin to see something more or less unprecedented in music history: musicians committed to radical and even revolutionary left politics.

Perhaps the first musician easily identifiable within this category was the German composer Hanns Eisler. Considered by Schoenberg his most brilliant student, Eisler would become radicalized in his early twenties, attempting to join the Communist Party (he was rejected for failing to pay his dues) and succeeding Kurt Weill as a collaborator with Berthold Brecht. Forced into exile in 1933, Eisler moved to New York City, where he exerted an influence on the members of the Composers Collective, which, like the Berlin-based November Group (of which Eisler was a member), consisted of artists more or less sympathetic to and operating under the auspices of the CP.

Among the Collective's membership, which included Henry Cowell (composer of "The Banshee" and other modernist classics), Marc Blitzstein (*The Cradle Will Rock*), Earl Robinson (*The Ballad of Americans*, "Joe Hill"), Alex North (*A Streetcar Named Desire*), was Aaron Copland, the best-known American composer of concert music. Copland's political trajectory during this period is representative of many in his generation.

John Halle

Already sympathetic to socialism through the candidacy and writings of Eugene Debs, upon returning to New York City from Paris in 1925 Copland belonged to artistic circles which, according to his biographer Howard Pollock, "identified strongly with 'the masses' and the 'proletariat' and spoke confidently of the coming 'revolution' and the collapse of 'bourgeois capitalism.'"

Along similar lines to other artists and writers associated with the cultural front, the Composers' Collective, according to Pollock, viewed themselves as seeking "to find a style of music appropriate to the Marxist revolution," though, not surprisingly, this style turned out to be not so easily identified or achieved. In theory, all sides agreed with Big Bill Heywood's adage that "nothing is too good for the working class." When it came to the arts generally and music in particular, the question of what "the best" was and who should determine it was hard to answer. One view, associated with Eisler and at least initially influential, was along traditional lines, taking high arts and culture generally in more or less their existing form as constituting a pinnacle of human achievement.[8] The revolution would view them as it would any of the feudal and haute bourgeoisie's most coveted possessions, as assets to be liberated and made available to the masses, just as one would a castle, its grounds, its Rembrandts and Velazquezes, or the crown jewels.

But it was also recognized that Eisler's vision required that working-class audiences be able to appreciate what was being provided for them, or at least a desire to achieve a requisite degree of conventional musical and cultural literacy. This entailed their being provided access to an education far above the rudimentary level that most had received. It should be understood that regarding a lack of familiarity or appreciation of the high arts as a form of impoverishment was not mere paternalism among the vanguardist elements of the leadership. That workers themselves recognized their experience of cultural deprivation and economic oppression as linked can be seen in Stanley Aronowitz's description of his working-class Jewish family as committed to "'high' art [as] the only possible cultural legacy for a working class that sought to transcend the degraded conditions of its subordinate existence."[9] While it would result in a rightward political trajectory in his case, journalist Joe Queenan observes along similar lines that it was "Because of my working-class background, [that] 'serious' music was important to me—not only because it was mysterious and beautiful in a way the Rolling Stones were not, but because it confirmed that I had cut my ties with the proletariat and 'arrived.'"[10]

• 123 •

The demand among workers for an education enabling them to transcend their cultural impoverishment was fulfilled by two different institutions within the organized left. One was the labor unions, which had then assumed, as has been observed, a much broader function in workers' lives, very different from the narrowly focused, legalistic bureaucracies they have since become. An indication can be seen in a 2006 newsgroup posting[11] from Upstate New York electrical worker Jerry Monaco:

> My Italian working-class neighborhood in an industrial town was ruled by General Electric, the Catholic Church, the democratic machine, and the union local. But the people in that neighborhood I remember from 1965 had a good eye for "the quality" of certain things—good food, of course, but also good music . . . My great grandfather could tell you why Verdi was good and Puccini was "like adding sugar to honey" and he never even finished the third grade. . . . My great Uncle Tony could tell you why Louis Armstrong was great . . . and why he liked Frank Sinatra and Billy Holiday but why so many other popular singers were "empty." Uncle Tony never graduated from high school, but he did take classes in classical music [at] the union hall. He belonged to a reading group at the union hall and read poetry. Yes there was a poetry group for the factory workers at the union hall in Schenectady, NY. I tend to think that because such people were around I learned to appreciate quality.

There is anecdotal evidence that Monaco's experience was not unusual: union halls fulfilled an important social, cultural, and educational function for many thousands of workers, though so far as I know, these have not been the subject of much scholarly attention.

Although the unions' role was substantial, probably more central in advancing workers' cultural education in the beginning of the 20th century were the now mostly forgotten workers schools operated under the sponsorship of the Communist Party. These, which included the Thomas Jefferson School for Social Science in New York, Samuel Adams School in Boston, Abraham Lincoln School in Chicago, Los Angeles People's Educational Center, and San Francisco Labor School, would spread to virtually every major city with a yearly enrollment of many thousands at their peak.[12]

While weighted toward the social sciences, economics, history, and sociology as taught from a Marxian perspective, a substantial humanities and arts curriculum was also available to students, with courses at the flagship Jefferson School in music history and music theory taught by composers such as Wallingford Riegger and Marc Blitzstein and by scholars such as Sidney Finkelstein and Charles Seeger. While these would be best described as music appreciation, that they were pitched at an atypically high level can be seen by the specialized topics covered, such as a class devoted to "the chamber music of Beethoven."[13] Additional evidence is provided by transcripts of the House Un-American Activities Committee making snide reference to classes taught by the distinguished emigré scholar Dr. Joachim Schumacher on "the bourgeois music culture in the period of monopoly capitalism"[14] and "the topography of Carl Maria Von Weber." Given the total enrollment, which in some years numbered as many as ten thousand, music classes at Jefferson School can reasonably be seen as having helped create a working-class presence among the core of enthusiasts for standard repertory works which was, at least until recently, a distinguishing feature of concert life of New York City.

In addition to its role in developing an appreciation for "the classics," what can be referred to as the organized left, that is, the Communist Party, along with its splinter parties and labor unions (some affiliated with the CP, others hostile to it) frequently used their facilities and publicity networks to present musical events. While only some of these featured classical musicians, the scale on which these occurred was impressive. One of the most important venues was the ILGWU's summer retreat, Unity House, whose 1,200-seat open-air concert hall, according to a pamphlet circulated at the time, featured "famous guest stars" in addition to orchestral programs performed by a "brilliant, permanent company of musicians." A 1938 *Life* magazine profile[15] of the "million dollar resort" suggests that it "would make a fine setting for a movie," describing a boy-meets-girl romance against the backdrop of "listening to string quartets" and the two-thousand-volume library. The union workers pictured in the issue look like nothing so much as present-day students at my own school (Bard College), privileged hipster sophisticates sporting wrap-around sunglasses, chinos, and sneakers. While probably a cynical attempt by *Life* and its publisher, the notorious media mogul Henry Luce, to promote the ILGWU as a bulwark against other more left-leaning unions, it is nonetheless revealing that *Life* presents union life as having achieved not only decent wages and working conditions for its members, but something approaching glamour.

What these anecdotes attest to is the organized left's having assumed a role not just as an inheritor but, to a significant extent, as a curator of artistic high culture. Furthermore, as mentioned earlier, it would be high culture along the most traditional, so-called Arnoldian lines, a reference to the Victorian figure Matthew Arnold, who famously described the arts as "the best which has been thought and said." The implicit statement conveyed by the left was that the kind of relationship of the arts with society that a reactionary nineteenth-century Eton headmaster envisions is not only not inconsistent with economic radicalism but that a workers' state offers its best hope for survival.[16] While subsequent decades offer conflicting evidence as to whether this was a reasonable status for the left to aspire to and whether it could assume it effectively, there is some evidence in its favor.

In particular, while much was amiss in the later years of the Soviet Union, in retrospect it can be seen as the last bastion of classical music in something approximating a traditional, viable, and even vibrant form: it was more or less unanimously conceded that the greatest virtuosi of the second half of the twentieth century—Richter, Oistrakh, and Rostropovich, among many others—were nurtured by the Soviet system and found a place as cultural icons within it. Furthermore, unlike the West, where postwar avant-garde composers tended to be relegated to the status of "uninvited guests to a dinner party," in the words of Polish composer Witold Lutoslawski, Soviet contemporary composers such as Shostakovich and Schnittke were honored by general audiences, their works being appreciated as at once contemporary and as a legitimate extension of the tradition, in sharp distinction to the attitudes of audiences toward the self-conscious "Year Zero" ideology promulgated by Western high modernists such as Pierre Boulez. Richard Taruskin's report of the premiere of the Shostakovich 15th Symphony describes the audience receiving the work as "a grateful, emotional salute to a cherished life companion, a fellow citizen and fellow sufferer, who had forged a mutually sustaining relationship with his public."[17] This was, according to Taruskin, "altogether outside the experience of any musician in my part of the world." In particular, it would be hard to imagine this reception applying to any Western composers of the postwar period, even the most celebrated, who were to some degree respected, but in an important sense not beloved.

Their seminal role within the Soviet Union notwithstanding, the Eislerian / Arnoldian vision of high arts within working class culture would not, ultimately, be sustained by left political formations in the West. Among the reasons for the decline was on the one side, intellectuals becoming increasingly aware of the climate of repression under Stalin, which extended to the targeting of artists, most notably Shostakovich. In response, most composers and musicians would abandon the Communist Party, fracturing their alliance with the working class under the cultural front umbrella, with most ultimately finding themselves somewhere on the spectrum from the liberal left to neo-conservative right. On the other side, the working class would not always be as open as Aronowitz and Monaco would have predicted to the attempts to provide them with cultural and artistic guidance. Among many indications, a consultant hired by the ILGWU to offer advice on programming at Unity House noted that "the working class patrons . . . did not care for the serious entertainment, nor did they want to be uplifted report[ing] that Unity House had too much culture, classical music, heavy drama, and surreal dancing. [He] suggested that it lighten up with lowbrow humor, dance contests, amateur nights and costume balls."[18] As the unions abandoned their commitment to high culture in the 1950s, composers moved in the other direction, viewing themselves, as noted in a widely circulated article[19] by Milton Babbitt, as "specialists" in an arcane technical discipline, who should no more make accommodations to popular tastes than would an algebraic topologist or quantum physicist. Predictably, it would not be long before the gap between working class and high musical culture would widen to the point that no bridge between the two would seem possible or even imaginable.

In retrospect, it appears obvious that the Eislerian / Arnoldian view could not survive the general resistance to the imposition of a high art that most found alien and an increasingly uncompromising and hermetic classical music establishment celebrating its refusal to be dictated to by an unsophisticated broad public. What would eventually supplant Eisler as the dominant musical philosophy informing not just the Communist Party, but the left across the board was one that would embrace and celebrate working-class musical culture, rather than repudiate it as alienated and degraded. This view would be associated with another Composers' Collective member, Charles Seeger, then a composer and musicologist, now best known as the father of Pete Seeger, who should be seen as functioning as a proselytizing Aaron to his father's Moses.

Whereas for Eisler the foundation of the new musical culture would remain recognized masterworks and the classical forms in which they were composed, the Seegers rejected elite, haute-bourgeois high arts as inherently undemocratic and authoritarian. Rather, what needed to be recognized and celebrated by the left were indigenous popular forms of music, which, while necessarily expressively impoverished and stunted by capitalism, would provide the foundation on which a rich proletarian musical culture would develop.

Among these indigenous styles was jazz, the urban, cosmopolitan variant, the subject of Seeger's *Daily Worker* colleague Sidney Finkelstein's *Jazz: A Peoples Music*, one of the first serious studies of the idiom, anticipating by many years its eventual institutionalization within university jazz studies departments and canonization by Ken Burns (among others) as "America's classical music." The rural variant was folk music, which Pete would passionately champion in a career of seven decades. Folk would become during the '50s culturally and commercially central, as groups such as the Weavers (of which Pete was a member) and then their well-scrubbed, depoliticized successors such as the Kingston Trio, New Christy Minstrels and Brothers Four, took their place on the hit parade.

The folk revolution would be succeeded in short order by rock, which would, to an even greater degree, define itself by its rejection of high art and elite culture: gone were traditional forms celebrated by Eisler, almost entirely vanished were extended, self-contained instrumental works, these replaced largely by songs, usually of dimensions appropriate for commercial airplay. Orchestral instruments would be displaced by the guitars inherited from the folk revolution, with amplified guitar becoming the vehicle for virtuosic displays of a familiar Liszt-Paganinian sort, albeit projected into stadiums holding audiences two orders of magnitude larger than those of the nineteenth century.

A more conspicuous and significant departure can be found in the extra-musical accouterments of the concert ritual. The new standards, which applied to both folk and rock, and the public's quick and enthusiastic acceptance of them were accurately described in a letter[20] to the New York *Times* from Grant Wiggins of Hopewell, N.J.: "For the past 40 years, rock has taught us that emoting and participating with our bodies and voices are part of the show. You can't do that in a concert hall. The entire society dresses informally now; concerts still involve formal wear by the audience, as if back in the 1890s."

As Mr. Wiggins suggests, not only would formal concert dress, tuxedos, evening gowns, high heels, and patent leather shoes be replaced by the worker's blue jeans, shirts, sneakers, or cowboy boots but also acculturated speech would be replaced by vernacular r-droppings, dipthongizations, "ain't," "wontcha," and "dontcha." Field hollers and screams of the evangelical church were imported for use both by the performers and audience. Most conspicuously, the repressed codes of behavior claimed by Levine as mechanisms to discipline a restive working class at the turn of the previous century would be jettisoned, with audiences now taking for granted active, as opposed to passive, participation in the concert ritual. All of this would be at least superficially consistent with Seeger's philosophy, if not to his liking, as will be discussed momentarily.

Before we engage this point, it is worth digressing to note that the replacement of haute-bourgeois standards of decorum by those associated, as least superficially, with the working class is often taken as a victory, the cultural equivalent of the storming of the winter palace or the sansculottes entering Versailles. But if this was a victory, it needs to be well understood that it was a tiny skirmish within a much larger war in which the devastation of the working class was virtually total. The indications of the defeat are by now so familiar as to barely require mentioning, among them, the aggregate wealth of the top 500 families exceeding that of the bottom 100 million, the decline of private (and now public sector) unions to single-digit levels reminiscent of the darkest, most Dickensian periods in industrial history, the leveling or even drop in life expectancy of lower-income groups over the past two decades, etc.[21]

Rather than merely registering a correlation, another possibility is along Eislerian lines, viewing the collapse of high musical culture as connected to the decline of the working class and its capacity to resist the elite campaign against it. That this explanation might seem dubious is indicated in part by the distance we have travelled from the Composers' Collective. Among the few who have been willing to link the collapse of the left's core agenda to the collapse in musical high culture is R. G. Davis who, in the late 1980s, attempted to rehabilitate Eisler in one of the initial issues of the seminal left journal *Rethinking Marxism*.[22]

In particular, Davis endorses Eisler's view that "simple music does and can reflect only simple political thinking." While conceding that they will not necessarily do so, "it is easier for people who appreciate complex music to move on to an appreciation of complex political problems, than

for those who limit themselves to folk (pop, rock, gospel, blues, etc.)."
Echoing Eisler's endorsement of the "rigorous methodology" of serial-
ism as "inherently anti-thetical to fascism," Davis argues that the "sonata
form [which] entertains two thoughts working simultaneously" embodies
a "Hegelian . . . notion of contradiction" and thereby can support a critical discourse. The "easy resolution of folk which has come down from
the 1930s into the 1980s via Charles Seeger and his followers is almost
always 'feel good' music . . . with only room for one theme and little for
oppositional dialogue." This is because

> the form of most folk and almost all jazz / pop music does not
> (cannot) even reflect industrial social relations as we know
> them, much less make a comment on them. Classical music,
> or music organized by a trained composer, art music, is more
> likely to produce an instructional metaphor (and form) with
> which to examine the foundations of corporate society.

While I would not necessarily endorse it, Davis's equation of "easy listening" with the easy platitudes of corporate public relations and government press releases propagated through the commercial media seems
reasonable enough. A bit more of a stretch, but certainly worth considering, is Davis's metaphor relating the habits of thought necessary to grasp
the logic of an extended composition, say, Sibelius's Fifth Symphony, with
the sort of critical engagement required to make sense of the systems of
hierarchy and control in complex political economies.

It probably won't come as a surprise that Davis's article made little impact,
and was likely regarded by the few who read it as somewhat eccentric.
The reason for this returns us to Seeger and the basic outlines of the
Seegerian philosophy. In particular it requires the recognition that these
have by now achieved a nearly hegemonic status in popular consciousness—including among the left. Eclecticism of the sort endorsed by both
Seegers now reigns supreme, all musical genres are equally worthy of celebration, and assumed, when subject to the form of analysis appropriate
to the genre, to inevitably reveal considerable and sometimes astounding
subtlety and sophistication (as will any human language, as the field of
linguistics has demonstrated[23]). This provides the grounds for taking as
established truth Duke Ellington's remark that all styles are equally able
to produce the only two meaningfully distinguishable types of music:

good and bad. And with this comes the corollary that musicologist Robert Fink advanced more than a decade and half ago and worth restating here, that classical music is by now "one style among many and by no means the most prestigious."

Accepting Ellington leaves Eisler and the Eislerians on shaky ground—proselytizers for a self-important elite agenda that bore some resemblance to the vanguardist intolerance that would be a notably unattractive feature of the state socialist regimes that many of them endorsed, reluctantly or otherwise. From this follows the rather underwhelming conclusion that rather than escaping their class to the greener fields of high culture, the workers could have got what they wanted by staying where they were. Stanley Aronowitz's father and Jerry Monaco's uncle had no reason to feel deprived in the first place. The education they received could have been better directed to an appreciation of what they already possessed. Rather than climbing the high-culture mountain, they could have got to the summit by driving their air-conditioned Impalas up the other side.

To the extent that the demise of musical high culture and the elevation of popular forms, both in terms of their prestige and their nearly complete domination of the musical marketplace, constitute a triumph, Seeger has triumphed. But it is by no means clear that Seeger himself would have regarded it as such. One indication to the contrary is provided by an iconic moment within rock history, the 1965 Newport Folk Festival at which Dylan made his final break with unamplified folk music, assaulting the audience with a maximal volume "Maggie's Farm." Charles, nearly 80, accompanied Pete. And while accounts of Pete's hostility to amplified rock are likely highly exaggerated by Dylan fans wanting to construe a Seeger-Dylan standoff in mythic, Oedipal terms, Charles likely did have misgivings, with respect to both Dylan's performance and the form that the rock revolution ultimately took.

To recognize what these may have been requires looking more closely at Seeger's stated views, which are somewhat subtler than Davis's critique of them would suggest. One statement is contained in a memo[24] Seeger wrote in his capacity as director of the WPA Federal Music Project, overseeing those working under the FMP's auspices. Most prominently, Seeger will be seen to promote a horizontalist musical culture, privileging active participation in music above passive listening: the former is the "essential thing," whereas the later was "secondary," according to him.

Complementing this was a rejection of the peaks of musical achievement, i.e. the production of masterpieces as the standard by which musical culture should be judged:

> "As every person is musical . . . [t]he musical culture of the nation is to be estimated upon the extent of participation of the whole population rather than upon the extent of the virtuosity of a fraction of it."

And given that "music as a group activity is more important than music as individual accomplishment," "professional music" should not be "artificially stimulated." Finally, perhaps most challenging of all, Seeger wasn't interested in whether a piece of music was or was not, in some sense, "good"; rather he was interested in "what is it good for?"

These amount to a direct attack on the Eislerian vision of the high musical arts, albeit of a familiar sort. The "artificial stimulation" Seeger refers to implicates the many years of subsidized, formal training that are necessary for classical musicians; in contrast, the skills required to perform in most other styles are learned "on the job," mainly by performing and socially engaging with others. The subsidies are justifiable if one assumes that the masterpieces of the literate medium have a unique, transcendent value.

This assumption is challenged by Seeger, raising doubts as to whether the question of musical quality—"what is good"—is even meaningful in the absence of an understanding of what is gained by defining a hierarchy of musical value—"what is it good for?" Asking the latter question turns back on itself classical music's commitment to "timeless masterpieces," equating these to an economy similarly hierarchically organized albeit around the production of concentrations of wealth and power. How can we criticize one, and celebrate the other? Seeger quite reasonably asks the left.

The implications of Seeger's horizontalism, its rejection of rigid hierarchies of taste defined by the traditional, sacralized canon, its devalorization of elegantly clad celebrity conductors, singers, and instrumentalists, its deflation of the pomposity of traditional concert music rituals are of a piece with a populist left critique particularly applicable to a self-improvement oriented, Mortimer Adler–reading bourgeoisie of the 1950s. But a minute's thought will reveal that what was intended as an attack on musical culture of the previous century dominated by the classics is just as applicable to the contemporary musical hierarchy, in which the classical canon has little to no place. Most conspicuously, music has for years been dominated by a hierarchy of stars with a more-or-less comparable public profile and social status to Liszt, Caruso, Bernstein, or Paganini. And music fans are obsessed with what they take, unproblematically, to be "the best," relying on objective rankings systems such the top 40, YouTube hits, or downloads as proxies for quality. Rock critics such as Chuck Klosterman and Ken Ward, by now far more numerous and visible than the Olin Downeses and Harold Rosenbaums of the last century, argue passionately over elaborate and subtle points of interpretation within what has become a sacralized rock music canon.

Classical music competitions—the Queen Elizabeth, Tchaikovsky, and Naumberg—have somehow limped on into the new century, but by now much more prominent are their farcical repetitions in the form of *American Idol* and its assorted spin-offs. And while musicians tend not to have traditional conservatory educations, rock is thoroughly professionalized, with layers of highly trained studio engineers, video technicians, legal staffs, and marketing and sales personnel engaged in the promotion and distribution of what is a major commercial product.

Furthermore, now that conventional musical literacy no longer poses a barrier, there is considerable room for amateur participation in music making, though it is not obvious that it is of a sort which the Seegers would have had much affinity with. For it is likely that the advance of communications technologies, having made professionally produced music available for free to all those who want it, has made for a less participatory music culture, with the production, as opposed to the consumption, left to those who have successfully negotiated the obstacles of the commercial marketplace. Performing music, which used to mean manipulating the eighty-eight keys of a keyboard or the six strings of the guitar, now tends to mean entering the sequences of keystrokes necessary to download an MP3 on I-tunes. DJs have now blurred the boundaries of the skills required of the performing musician with that of the listener. Is this really the kind of participation Seeger envisioned, or is it nothing more than a slightly elevated form of passive engagement?

All this should be sufficient to demonstrate that, with the exception of a few minor points of overlap, both Seeger's and Eisler's visions of a proletarian musical culture are far distant from where we are now, as is the broader social and economic transformation that both were committed to. What has triumphed is, of course, capitalism, and within it a musical culture reflecting the dominance of markets as much as, if not more than, in other aspects of society.

It is in this light that the mid-century musical culture wars should be seen. For a brief period, the counter-hegemonic potential of Seegerian musical styles (folk and rock) was realized and played a role in the mass movements of the sixties. But it soon became clear that a part of the foundation on which they were constructed would be unable to support the aspirations that were projected onto it. For just as workers themselves suffer from what Richard Sennett and Jonathan Cobb in their classic study[25] call "the hidden injuries of class" so too does working-class culture reflect the routine degradation, tedium, and imposed ignorance that the Aronowitz and Monaco families were committed to escaping. Eventually, what was taken initially as transgressive political content turned out to be no more than another circus provided by elites in exchange for ever-diminishing bread. Worse, the "revolution" in musical style that resulted in the global hegemony of rock music was celebrated by the right as a validation of capitalism's transcendent virtues.

This among other indications would seem sufficient to validate Eisler's equation of simple music with the toxic simple truths of public relations and capitalist "common sense." With capitalism now in deep crisis, it might appear to those of us whose musical lives have been committed to preserving the sonatas, variations, minuets, and fugues that Eisler claims should constitute the foundation of an oppositional musical culture that our time has finally come. But any optimism along these lines should be combined with the critical Seegerian awareness that elite, haute-bourgeois musical culture can be, and usually is, deeply alienating to those outside its walls and is often designed to achieve precisely this end.

Related to this is the increasing awareness that reports of the demise of classical music are now no longer exaggerated, at least in the sense of its having become a dead language—its repertoire of gestures, inventory of timbres, limited formal road maps and performance rituals leaving it largely unable to communicate to audiences other than the most geriatric. All that tells us what we already know: our project is to build a new world either on the foundations of the old or, more likely, if the past is any guide, somewhere else entirely. We should be doing it everywhere—in and outside of music.

NOTES

1. This piece had its origins in a talk at the James Connolly Forum in Troy, New York, on March 15, 2013. I would like to thank Connolly Forum director Jon Flanders for the invitation to speak, and the Connolly Forum audience for questions that precipitated many of the ideas discussed herein. Also, thanks to Anton Vishio, Karl Lerud, Mark Mishler, Noam Chomsky, and Alex Ross for commenting on the draft.

2. John Halle, "Occupy Wall Street: Composers and the Plutocracy," *New Politics* (14/1 2012): 85-96. http://newpol.org/content/occupy-wall-street-composers-and-plutocracy-some-variations-ancient-theme.

3. Lawrence Levine, *Highbrow / Lowbrow: The Emergence of Cultural Hierarchy in America* (Cambridge, MA: Harvard University Press, 1990).

4. Michael Denning, *The Cultural Front: The Laboring of American Culture in the Twentieth Century* (London: Verso, 1996).

5. I am indebted to Anton Vishio and Alex Ross for reminding me of this oversight in an earlier draft.

6. See http://socialjusticefirst.com/2013/05/22/wagners-200th-birthday-his-politics-his-music-and-the-ring/ for an excellent discussion of Wagner's political commitments and alliances.

7. E.g., Schoenberg described himself as a "royalist," and Stravinsky expressed "veneration" for Mussolini, as did Webern (somewhat more ambiguously) for "this unique man" Hitler.

8. For Eisler's views on these matters, see James Wierzbicki, "Hanns Eisler and the FBI," *Music and Politics* (2/2: 2011), and R. G. Davis, "Music from the Left," *Rethinking Marxism* (Winter 1988): 7–25.

9. Stanley Aronowitz, *Roll over Beethoven: The Return of Cultural Strife,* (Hanover, NH: University Press of New England, 1993), 107.

10. http://www.guardian.co.uk/music/2008/jul/09/classicalmusicandopera.culture.

11. http://mailman.lbo-talk.org/2007/2007-December/023833.html.

12. I am grateful to Joel Kovel for bringing these remarkable institutions to my attention.

13. Marvin Gettleman, *Lost World of U.S. Labor Education: Curricula at East and West Coast Community Schools, 1944–1957,* available at http://www.gothamcenter.org/festival/2001/confpapers/gettleman.pdf.

14. http://archive.org/stream/investigationofc5701unit/investigationofc5701unit_djvu.txt.

15. "ILGWU: A Great and Good Union Points the Way for America's Labor Movement," *Life* Magazine (August 1, 1938): 45.

16. A concise formulation of the idea is attributed to the late journalist and labor scholar Robert Fitch: "The bourgeoisie takes very bad care of its cultural inheritance."

17. Richard Taruskin, "Double Trouble," *The New Republic,* (December 24, 2001): 26–34.

18. Lawrence Squeri, *Better in the Poconos: The Story of Pennsylvania's Vacationland* (University Park, PA: Pennsylvania State University Press, 2002).

19. Milton Babbitt, "Who Cares if You Listen?" *High Fidelity,* February 1958.

20. Grant Wiggins, letter to the editor, New York *Times,* November 25, 2012, http://www.nytimes.com/2012/11/25/opinion/sunday/sunday-dialogue-is-classical-music-dying.html.

21. Documentation provided in, for example, Jeff Madrick, *Age of Greed: The Triumph of Finance and the Decline of America, 1970 to the Present* (New York: Alfred A. Knopf, 2011).

22. R. G. Davis, "Music from the Left," *Rethinking Marxism* (Winter 1988): 7–25.

23. See, for example, Mark Baker, *The Atoms of Language: The Mind's Hidden Rules of Grammar* (New York: Basic Books, 2001).

24. Quoted in Pete Seeger, *Where Have All The Flowers Gone: A Singer's Stories, Songs, Seeds, Robberies* (Bethlehem, PA: Sing Out, 2005).

25. Richard Sennett and Jonathan Cobb, *The Hidden Injuries of Class* (Cambridge, UK: Cambridge University Press, 1972).

Science and Music:
Consonance or Dissonance?

MELVIN CHEN

The nature of the relationship between science and music has been discussed and debated since the ancient Greeks. There seems little common ground between the two, so why force a connection? After all, music is generally thought of as in the province of feeling and emotion, full of passion and irrationality. And science is precise and rational, concerned with adding knowledge about the ways in which our world works. Anecdotally, however, there are many examples of scientists who are avid musicians; to name but two examples, physicist Albert Einstein was a serious amateur violinist, and Dudley Herschbach, a Nobel laureate in chemistry, was an amateur clarinetist. The same is true in the other direction—the composer Alexander Borodin was a professional chemist, and other more recent performers have active scientific interests—the pianist Christopher Taylor comes to mind. Additionally, there has been considerable recent activity and research into the science of music and its associated particulars, including topics such as music cognition, acoustics, or effects of music on infant brain development. These topics, while valuable in their own way, seem somewhat unsatisfying as a way of connecting the two disciplines. In many of these cases, science is used to "explain" music, so that science is used in service of music. Similarly, there have been attempts by scientists and musicians to "visualize" science through music, like the project that created a sonic representation of DNA. In this case music is used in the service of science.

My aim in this essay is not to answer the question of what the relationship of music and science is or should be, but rather to examine commonalities between the two.

The process of interpreting a piece of music is simultaneously emotional and intellectual. A compelling performance of a work of music based purely on emotion cannot exist, because the feelings must be placed in context. The audience must understand on some level, if not explicitly, that there is a causal relationship between different feelings in a piece. Or if one character predominates, as in movements of Bach suites, the listener can differentiate variations or intensities of the character, and why and how we are moving through these states. The performer is in a curious role in all of this, as an intermediary between the composer and the listener. The performer has to make decisions about how to play the music based on several sources of information—the musical text itself, the performer's own reaction to the text, and other relevant information (the composer's biography, circumstances of composition, etc.).

The result of synthesizing all of this information is a decision about how to approach every note in the score. By asking questions of all the available sources of information, a performer can build an idea of how a piece of music should sound. For me, this process is similar to what a scientist does in producing experiments that elucidate specific aspects of a particular problem. Each experiment produces data that is an incomplete picture of a physical system. After a series of various experiments, the scientist combines the data to generate a possible description of the system that is consistent with the observations. Of course, the results of these two similar processes are quite different.

As a practical example, let's examine a piece, "Mercutio," from Prokofiev's *Ten Pieces from Romeo and Juliet* for solo piano, op. 75:

8. Меркуцио

Looking solely at the musical markings, there are many pieces of information that one can use to deduce the tempo and character of the piece. The first is the metronome specification of the piece, which is 160 to the quarter note, a very brisk speed. Second, the tempo is marked as *Allegro giocoso*, with *giocoso* the descriptive adjective, meaning merry or playful. Next, we also see (with the exception of a single measure) accents on the beginning of every bar. With the information presented thus far, one could think of this piece as lighthearted, playful, and rhythmically in one beat per bar.

Now we can turn to other clues that undermine this characterization. In the fifth measure of the piece is the marking *brusco* (brusque), which suggests a more sinister side to this playfulness. We can also take note of the title of this piece, "Mercutio," and go back to Shakespeare's play to find more information about this character. In the play we see that Mercutio is a witty, enthusiastic character who is a contrast to Romeo's moody nature. Mercutio is joking even to his last breath, which ends with a pun:

"Ask for me to-morrow, and you shall find me a grave man." (Shakespeare, 39) On the other hand, he bitterly blames both the Montagues and the Capulets for his death: "A plague o' both your houses!" (Shakespeare, 39)

Additionally, we can look at what Prokofiev writes in his initial scenario for the ballet. In Mercutio's dance, which in the ballet has the analogous music to the piano piece, Prokofiev writes: "Mercutio's dance, somewhat buffoonish (certainly in ¾)."

The description "buffoonish" seems to go beyond the word "giocoso" in describing a more physical, overt type of humor, as opposed to a more subtle kind of wittiness, which seems in accord with the accents present in the score. The second part of the description, "certainly in ¾," is hard to reconcile with other markings that have been discussed. The fast metronome marking makes hearing the 3 beats per bar quite difficult. There are accents at the beginning of every bar, which accentuates a 1-beat-per-bar rhythm.

What are the options for bringing these conflicting notions together? One is simply to prioritize—to choose to follow Prokofiev's wishes in the scenario, and to disregard the metronome marking. Another option is to attempt to perform all the markings even if they are contradictory— and it is up to the judgment of the performer as to whether the result is compelling.

In science, one can follow an analogous process to arrive at new knowledge. Given a set of experimental observations, the goal of the scientist is to arrive at an interpretation that is consistent with the data. One of the most famous examples of this comes from the beginning of quantum mechanics, specifically the conclusion that energy is quantized. At the beginning of the twentieth century, classical physics had advanced to the point that scientists were confident that their theories could be used to explain any observable phenomena. However, two examples in particular contradicted this belief. The first is what is now commonly referred to as the "ultraviolet catastrophe." This refers to the radiation emitted by a blackbody, an ideal substance at a constant temperature that absorbs all wavelengths of light. The spectrum of radiation emitted by a blackbody is governed in classical mechanics by the Rayleigh-Jeans law, which postulated that the energy emitted by a blackbody was inversely proportional to the fourth power of the wavelength. Clearly there is a problem, because the energy emitted goes to infinity as the wavelength approaches zero. Experimentally, energy was observed to remain finite at shorter wavelengths.

At around the same time, the photoelectric effect was also being discussed. This effect refers to the fact that electrons are ejected from many metal surfaces when irradiated by light. The rate and number of electrons was shown to depend on both the frequency and the amplitude of light. There were two unexplained deviations from the classical predictions, however. First, classically one would expect the ejected electrons to vary in their kinetic energy depending on the intensity of the light: that is, the more intense the light, the more energetic the electrons that are ejected. This is not what was observed, however; instead, the energy of the emitted electrons was found to be independent of intensity. The electrons had the same energy, whether the light was weak or strong. Second, there was a threshold frequency—light that was shined on the metal below this frequency, no matter the intensity, no electrons would be ejected. These two observations went completely against the classical understanding of energy, and could not be explained within this model.

Classically, light was understood as a wave. In fact, the understanding of the wave properties of light was developed by first understanding the wave properties of sound, especially as related to the sound production of musical instruments. The visible spectrum of light was described initially as analogous to the musical intervals, with the fundamental ratio of 2:1 as the interval of an octave, with the other smaller intervals as other integer ratios. It later turned out that the "interval" of the visible spectrum is a major sixth, but the study of sound waves inspired and informed the later study of light waves. Albert Einstein was one of the first scientists to solve the problem of the photoelectric effect. In the introduction to an article in which he posits the solution to these problems, he writes:

> It seems to me that the observation associated with black body radiation, fluorescence, the photoelectric effect, and other related phenomena associated with the emission or transformation of light are more readily understood if one assumes that the energy of light is discontinuously distributed in space. (Arons, 368)

He suggests that light energy is produced in the form of discrete quanta of energy, as opposed to a continuous distribution, and suggests that light has aspects of a particle. This conclusion is a shocking one, because it goes completely against everything thought of in classical mechanics. However, using this assumption, one has a model that explains all of the inconsistencies observed in the ultraviolet catastrophe and the photoelectric effect. And from this simple but unintuitive assumption the new physics of quantum mechanics is developed, a theory that shows that the world behaves radically differently from previously thought at small-length scales. As the length scale increases, the quantum world becomes the classical world that had been previously well understood.

In comparing the admittedly quite different cases of the interpretation of a piece from Prokofiev and the discovery of the quantization of energy, one can see that both require the collecting of data and the search for an interpretation compatible with the data, as well as the use of deductive reasoning. In music, though, this process is merely a guide toward an interpretation. One can choose to ignore certain things, and still have a convincing performance. It is my opinion, however, that by considering all aspects of a work of music, the bond between composer, performer, and audience is strengthened. Certainly, it is difficult to pull off an interpretation that goes against the ideas that the composer had in mind, but it is not impossible. In science these constraints are much more rigid. In attempting to formulate a precise and clear understanding of natural phenomena, any successful model must accurately explain all inconsistencies observed experimentally. There is no choosing among observations or ideas that contradict a given hypothesis—all must be suitably explained!

While the scientist has additional responsibilities to the data at hand, essentially the job of musician and scientist are, at their best, creative ones. Clearly, certain composers are creative geniuses—Bach, for being able to create works of such beauty and complexity, and Beethoven in the way that he pushed the bounds of traditional structure. But there are also performers of similar creativity—Glenn Gould comes to mind, as one whose singular interpretations changed the way Bach was heard from that point on. As a scientist, Einstein makes creative mental leaps that parallel those of Bach, Beethoven, and Gould. Although the idea of quantization of energy did not originate solely with Einstein, he had other ideas that can be regarded as astonishingly creative, such as the theory of special relativity. Similarly, other great scientists demonstrate this sort of creativity—the ability to produce truly new ideas that are not simply logical extensions of existing concepts.

Scientists have begun exploring the concept of art in the natural world and its connection with human art. Are humans exceptional in their ability to create and appreciate art and music? Certainly bird songs offer many styles and even virtuosity, and animals exhibit what we might consider beautiful markings or aesthetically motivated behaviors. Evolutionary biologist Richard Prum has proposed that in fact aesthetics, evolution, and biology are inextricably linked. If this is true, then all art, including music, has a development that is simultaneous with human development in a biological and evolutionary sense. In this model the study of art and music is part of the scientific study of a species. Prum goes further, to say that in fact an aesthetic sense has evolved with many other species, including flowers, butterflies, and birds. Darwin, writing in *The Descent of Man*, espouses an explicitly aesthetic view of sexual selection of male birds by females:

> If female birds had been incapable of appreciating the beautiful colours, the ornaments, and voices of their male partners, all the labour and anxiety by the latter in displaying their charms before the females would have been thrown away, and this is impossible to admit . . . on the whole, birds appear to be the most aesthetic of all animals, excepting of course man, and they have nearly the same taste for the beautiful as we have. (Darwin, 61)

This aspect of Darwin's evolutionary theory had been ignored for almost a century. The main objection to the aesthetic argument is that *all* traits, including coloration patterns and bird song, are subject to natural selection, so that the "best" patterns and songs are the ones linked to better survival. This objection stems from an ancient and long-held idea of human exceptionalism—that humans are the only species capable of making aesthetic judgments about beauty. Prum's argument is that these successful secondary display traits are not necessarily indicative of better fitness, but rather are simply aesthetic qualities that are deemed attractive. These qualities co-evolve as the result of a feedback loop between artistic pioneers and "consumers." He proposes that this concept applies to the evolution of human art as well. In this way, humans are not exceptional in their ability to demonstrate aesthetic appreciation; rather, our art is simply a continuation of natural processes that have been present for a long time.

It is worth asking, after all this, whether there is any real relationship that we should recognize between science and music. Historically, music was included by Plato, along with arithmetic, geometry, and astronomy, as the secondary part of the curriculum of the guardians in the Republic. These four subjects were called the "quadrivium" by later Latin authors and became essential parts of the "liberal arts." Music, arithmetic, geometry and astronomy formed the basis of knowledge in mathematics. Specifically, music was concerned with distances between numbers, namely intervals. The Greeks were interested in the intervals expressed as specific ratios of frequencies, and the harmony that resulted from these ratios. This concept was extended, especially by astronomers such as Kepler and Galileo, who took the phrase "the music of the spheres" as more than a metaphor and truly believed that the harmony of the planets moving was equivalent to the pleasing harmony one hears when two notes of different frequencies are played together to form a consonant interval.

Simultaneous to this use of music in science, the field of music was developing as a way to evoke feeling, first as primarily religious, and then for secular dance, for example. As time went on, music was viewed less by scientists as a way of examining spaces between numbers (especially since there was no way to express irrational numbers this way). And musicians in the eighteenth and nineteenth centuries were less concerned with music as a science and more interested in music as a form of expression. Music moved away from science and became closer to arts such as poetry or literature. And despite the inordinate number of scientists who happen to love and play music, perhaps there is no deep link on a fundamental level between the two disciplines. Rather than forcing an artificial connection, perhaps it is sufficient to appreciate and enjoy the thinking and learning that is required in both of these fields.

My own feeling about the relationship between science and music is perhaps best expressed by Einstein's remark on this subject: "Music does not influence research work, but both are nourished by the same sort of longing, and they complement each other in the release they offer." (Einstein, 78)

REFERENCES

A. B. Arons and M. B. Peppard, "Einstein's Proposal of the Photon Concept—A Translation of the Annalen der Physik Paper of 1905." American Journal of Physics 33.5 (1965): 367–374.

Charles Darwin, *The Descent of Man, and Selection in Relation to Sex* (New York: D. Appleton and Company, 1872).

Albert Einstein, Helen Dukas, and Banesh Hoffmann, *Albert Einstein, the Human Side: Glimpses from His Archives* (Princeton University Press, 2013).

Peter Pesic, *Music and the Making of Modern Science* (The MIT Press, 2014).

Sergei Prokofiev, *Romeo and Juliet*, original scenario, from Simon Morrison.

Richard O. Prum, "Aesthetic evolution by mate choice: Darwin's really dangerous idea." Philosophical Transactions of the Royal Society B: Biological Sciences 367.1600 (2012): 2253–2265.

Richard O. Prum, "Coevolutionary aesthetics in human and biotic artworlds." Biology & Philosophy 28.5 (2013): 811-832.

William Shakespeare, *Romeo and Juliet* (London: W. P. Nimmo, Hay & Mitchell, 1900).

The Animated Soldier

R. O. BLECHMAN

The eponymous soldier in Igor Stravinsky's *The Soldier's Tale* began his long journey in an unusual way and in an unusual place.

In 1974 I was invited to attend the Robert Flaherty Seminar in Milan, a gathering of documentary filmmakers. On the second day I met the program director of PBS at the hotel where we were both staying. "I loved your program," she said, referring to a previous PBS animated film of mine, *Simple Gifts*. "I just loved it. Are you thinking of any new projects for us?" Taken aback by her enthusiasm, I sputtered my thanks and something about how I would like to do another film, but had no projects in mind.

"Well, if you do, you'll let me know, please, won't you?"

"Won't I? " Well, why *didn't* I? Why didn't I tell her that I had *several* ideas. And here I had flubbed an ideal occasion to present them.

Leaving the hotel, walking more face down than up, I happened to pass (face up) La Scala Opera House. And there it was! A poster for Stravinsky's *The Soldier's Tale*. I knew that opera, and admired it immensely, so the thought occurred to me, "Why not an animated version of *The Soldier's Tale*?" A day later I met the program director of PBS and mentioned it to her.

"Yes, that's a wonderful idea. I love that opera!"

Apparently she had mounted a successful production of it when she was program director of the Walker Art Center in Minneapolis. "Do send me a proposal."

That was less than the response I hoped for, but I sent her a proposal—as much a pro forma response as anything else.

Several months passed. Without word from PBS, I forgot about the project. Forgot about it, that is, until I received a telephone call from WGBH, the Boston Public television station. They had been forwarded my proposal from Washington. WGBH was planning a four-hour

Stravinsky program on the occasion of his upcoming centenary. They had seen my proposal, liked it, and wanted to make my film one of their four segments.

So began the soldier's journey from Milan to the silver screen. From the zigs and zags of fate—from my visit to Milan, my encounter with the PBS program director, the poster at La Scala, and the upcoming Stravinsky centenary—a film was born.

I was given $20,000 to create a storyboard, but I decided to go for broke (a move that might have been as much literal as figurative) and began actual production of the animation, working to a recording by Gerard Schwarz—this, without any guarantee of full funding. As it happened, WGBH never did find sufficient funds for their ambitious four-part series, but since my segment was the only one already in production, the station sponsored it.

My soldier took his first steps.

Animation—at least its 2-D version—is expensive to produce. It's very much a hand-driven process involving animators who create drawing after drawing to simulate movement. Their drawings are usually in the form of key poses, which then go to "in-betweeners" who, as their name implies, take the animators' key drawings and fill them in to create the final movement. However, many animators prefer to do their own in-betweens. Like parents with newborn children, they don't want others to raise their creations.

In the production of *The Soldier's Tale*, several animators went beyond merely moving the characters, the layman's take on their function. The most creative animators are storytellers in their own right, using an artist's characters to create scenarios of their own devising.

I'm reminded of the time I called an animator friend of mine to tell him how much I admired Ralph Bakshi's 1978 animated film, *Heavy Traffic*, especially one particular episode.

"Which one?" my friend asked.

I mentioned a scene in a men's lavatory—a long pan across urinals, set to the music of Vivaldi; as startling and bizarre a musical choice as Kubrick's Johann Strauss waltz in *2001: A Space Odyssey*.[1]

"Thank you," my friend said, when I mentioned that episode.

"Why 'thank you'?" I asked.

"Because I created that scene."

I didn't question him, because my experience was that some animators, like my animator friend, are dramatists, scene makers, storytellers—not merely artists who move characters around. In the making of *The Soldier's Tale*, these animators created episodes to a great extent of their own devising.

Yes, I had discussed the episodes with them, and yes, I had given the animators model drawings, but then, like ad-libbing actors, they improvised the moves, the transitions, the editing. In effect, they had become my fellow directors.

One of these special animators was the late Tissa David. With her ability to read music, her animation was guided by the Stravinsky score—and she did not miss a beat, literally and figuratively. One of her remarkable creations was set to the strains of a tango. It featured a radio announcer, morphed into the Devil, who triumphantly seizes the soldier's violin. The violin, however, morphs in turn to become an avenging femme fatale—a machine-like creature who electrocutes him.[2]

Alongside Tissa David, another animator who greatly enhanced *The Soldier's Tale* was Ed Smith, a master draughtsman. In *Simple Gifts*, my hour-long PBS holiday special, which consisted of six segments styled by different illustrators, Smith animated almost the entire thirteen minutes of my segment, *No Room at the Inn*, a retelling of the Christmas story. Nobody else could have rendered horses and Herod, ducks and peasants, Joseph and Mary, with such balletic grace. Nobody else could have created drama and beauty out of simple wind-blown snow.

To return to the animation process: after a storyboard is drawn, a sound track is created—the voices, the music (in this case, a given), and often the sound effects, although these can be recorded later. For *The Soldier's Tale* I cast European voices—Max von Sydow as the Devil; German-born Brother Theodore as the drill master; Russian ballerina Galina Panova as the Princess; and Yugoslav film director Dusan Makaveyev as the Soldier—and what a perfect voice he had, cracking and vulnerable due to a recent throat operation. The only casting problem I had was to find an actor for the voiceover narration. Given the all-European voices, I knew that the narrator couldn't be an American or European voice . . . but somehow neither, yet both. A problem.

I took that problem home with me one evening.

"You're late for dinner," my wife said.

Dinner . . . dinner . . .

Then the voice I was looking for jumped out at me. Of course. I had recently seen a film, *My Dinner with André*. And there it was. André Gregory. The perfect transatlantic voice.

But I am ahead of myself. Back to the steps in making an animated film.

The storyboard, consisting entirely of my drawings, but occasionally with a scene by Tissa David, is filmed to provide the overall timing and action of the film. In a way, it *is* the film, only in rough shape, without the ultimate finesses.

With the line—or pencil—test completed, now was the time to edit the rough cut.

I noticed that the soldier's march that began the Stravinsky score was composed to a staccato four-four beat. This tempo exactly (and accidentally) corresponded to the line test I had filmed of the soldier's walk, so rather than filling out the animation to something smoother and more realistic, I kept the four-four beat for the entire several minutes of the film opening. The synchronicity of the music to the film was perfect. This was one of the many instances where the Stravinsky score dictated the timing of the animation.

Although music was invariably synchronous to the animation in *The Soldier's Tale*, this was not the case with the film's introduction—vintage photographs of World War I. The photographs began with images of smiling soldiers, confident that the war would end decisively and quickly. *Gott mit Uns*, the belt buckles of German soldiers assured them—so how could Germany lose with an ally like Him? In the opening montage of jauntily marching soldiers, the editing and music were perfectly synchronized (Stravinsky's Great Chorale, performed on the piano). But as the war dragged on, as victory seemed farther and farther away, the editing increasingly, but subtly, almost imperceptibly, missed the musical beat. This mismatch of image and sound undoubtedly created a tension—probably subliminal, but no less effective—for the audience.

Not all the music in the film was Stravinsky's. In one episode, where the soldier with his newfound wealth dines in San Simeon splendor (my homage to *Citizen Kane*), a pianist entertains the soldier with some off-key *tafelmusik* that I commissioned.

The use of outside music was perfectly appropriate in an opera unique in its heterogeneous musical riffs—waltz, jazz, marching tunes, ragtime, a paso doble, even a Dies Irae, and to my ears, a hint of Bach. This musical stew of Stravinsky was an invitation, not to be ignored—an invitation for me to experiment with different visual styles (Russian Constructivism for the soldier's crack-up; Expressionism for the soldier's ill-fated flight past the devil's boundaries; the opulent art of Maxfield Parrish, that dean of Golden Age illustration, for the soldier's visit to a new kingdom;

Joan Miro, where sunlit sparkles cast their reflections on a pond, etc. This was a compendium of art produced virtually in the same period as Stravinsky's score. Corresponding to the different visual styles were the different media I employed—pen, pencil, crayon, gouache, watercolor, airbrush, and collage.

This then, is the backstory of *The Soldier's Tale*, an opera whose free-wheeling music and storyline of Stravinsky and Ramuz offered—no, invited!—the creation of a wholly new scenario and visual treatment.

Walter Pater declared, "All art constantly aspires to the condition of music." The themes, the variations, the modulations in music—these all have counterparts in literature, painting, ballet, and other art forms. Consider William Shakespeare. He mixed the colloquial with the Latinate, Elizabethan vocabulary with neologisms—words he freely coined. Shakespeare created upwards of 1,500 new words—expressions like "Gadzooks!" referring to the nails, or hooks—"God's hooks"—in the Crucifixion. He used onomatopoeia extensively—words that sound like what they mean.

Hemingway used onomatopoeia in *For Whom the Bell Tolls* (I italicize these words): "He saw nothing, but he could feel his heart pounding, and then he heard the *clack* on stone and the leaping *click* of a small rock falling,"

Click, clack—pure onomatopoeia. Shakespeare, Hemingway, Virginia Woolf—the list could go on and on—all great writers have been composers and conductors of their own verbal orchestras.

Painters, likewise, play with rhythm and time. Using the vocabulary of color, hue, placement, and size, the artist's brush guides the viewer from one painted area to another. Aware that we in the West read from left to right, the artist takes advantage of this natural sequence to guide the viewer's eye. Alfred Hitchcock took advantage of this in his films. He had his heroes enter from left to right—his villains, from right to left.

But nowhere do these art forms share the *temporal* quality that film affords. Only film has short and long dissolves, zooms, pans, smooth cuts and jump cuts, deep focus shots (used so brilliantly in *Citizen Kane*, and to such great appreciation by Orson Welles that he wanted to give as much screen credit to the photographer, Greg Tolland, as to himself). And no genre of film offers the limitless possibilities that animation provides, with its ability to play freely with the drawn image as well as employ virtually all art media.

I'm convinced that nothing could have captured the freewheeling spirit of *The Soldier's Tale* as effectively as animation, with its unique graphic capabilities. I think of William Kentridge's animated flights of fantasy for the Met's production of Shostakovich's *The Nose*—a visual treatment so stunningly inventive that I am tempted to refer to the Met production not as Shostakovich's *The Nose*, but as William Kentridge's.

If my film ever gets known as Blechman's *L'Histoire* (*peace*, William Kentridge), it is because of a stroll in Milan, a poster at La Scala, a fortuitous centenary, but above all, the fact that a fabulous tail (music) got to wag a dog (my film).

NOTES

1. Composers, like animators, are too often neglected, and can play a hidden but significant role in films. In the 1939 Eisenstein film, *Alexander Nevsky*, the panorama of an advancing Russian army was accompanied, not by the sound of marching feet, but by Prokofiev's score with its propulsive accelerating beat. That scene was a great moment in cinematic history

2. Technology, throughout *The Soldier's Tale*, is a villainous leitmotif. Hell is set in the clouds, above the earth, not below it. The Devil's realm is a technological Heaven. In the final scene the Devil is seen in a war room reminiscent of *Dr. Strangelove*. Seated at his control panel, he destroys the soldier—and the world—in a technological apocalypse.

Contributors

André Aciman is Distinguished Professor of Comparative Literature at the Graduate Center of City University of New York.

Deborah Berke is the founder of Deborah Berke Partners and dean of the Yale School of Architecture.

R. O. Blechman is an animator, illustrator, children's-book author, graphic novelist, and editorial cartoonist.

Allegra Chapman is a 2010 graduate of the Bard College Conservatory of Music.

Melvin Chen is deputy dean and a member of the piano faculty of the Yale School of Music.

Ádám Fischer is a Hungarian conductor. He is the general music director of the Austro-Hungarian Haydn Orchestra, music director of the Hungarian Radio Symphony Orchestra, and chief conductor of the Danish National Chamber Orchestra.

Rylan Gajek-Leonard is a 2016 graduate of the Bard College Conservatory of Music.

John Halle is director of studies in music theory and practice at the Bard College Conservatory of Music.

Swapan S. Jain is associate professor of chemistry at Bard College.

Robert Kelly is Asher B. Edelman Professor of Literature at Bard College.

Peter Laki is visiting associate professor of music at Bard College.

Robert Martin is director of the Bard College Conservatory of Music and professor of music and philosophy and vice president for policy and planning at Bard College.

Jerrold Seigel is professor of history emeritus and William J. Kenan Jr. Professor of History at New York University.

Dawn Upshaw is artistic director of the Graduate Vocal Arts Program of the Bard College Conservatory of Music and Charles Franklin Kellogg and Grace E. Ramsey Kellogg Professor of the Arts and Humanities at Bard College.

The Richard B. Fisher Center for the Performing Arts at Bard College
Photo: ©Peter Aaron '68/Esto

Bard College Conservatory Orchestra in Sosnoff Theater,
The Richard B. Fisher Center for the Performing Arts at Bard College
Photo: Karl Rabe

László Z. Bitó '60 Conservatory Building
Photo: Chris Cooper, courtesy Deborah Berke Partners

László Z. Bitó '60 Conservatory Building atrium
Photo: Chris Cooper, courtesy Deborah Berke Partners

Student-faculty chamber music performance in Sosnoff Theater,
The Richard B. Fisher Center for the Performing Arts at Bard College
Photo: Karl Rabe

Bard College Conservatory Orchestra at Mariinsky Theatre,
St. Petersburg, Russia, during the 2014 concert tour
Photo: Classical Movements

Bard College Conservatory Orchestra at National University
of the Arts in Taipei, Taiwan, during the 2012 concert tour
Photo: Sina News

Bard College Conservatory Orchestra at
Konzerthaus Berlin in Germany during the 2014 concert tour
Photo: Classical Movements

Bard College Conservatory Orchestra members with concert tour
patrons and staff in Havana, Cuba, during the June 2016 concert tour
Photo: Laura Errabakh

Bard College Conservatory Orchestra with soloist Peter Serkin at
the Teatro Nacional de Cuba in Havana during the 2016 concert tour
Photo: Noemi Sallai